Mrs. O'Leary's Boarding House: Aliens Only

W. F. Halsey

Speculation Press Original

Cover by Judy Bullard

Dedicated to my grandmother, Martha Halsey, who ran a boarding house in Austin District of Chicago until 1961. The house described is her house which was built prior to 1860.

Stories

A Problem Guest

Katie O'Leary knocked the largest of the blue slugs back down into the pot of boiling water and gave the salty mixture a bit of a stir. Just a moment or two longer and then she'd scoop them out. Mr. Smzch didn't like his slugs over cooked.

Pushing a few strands of sweat-dampened copper-colored hair back from her forehead, Mrs. O'Leary reached for a large bowl. Her corset chafed and her skirt clung to her legs. A hot August it was, and maybe a little too much wood in the stove.

"Auntie!"

Oh dear, what had the girl found now?

"There's a gentleman at the door. He's heard we've rooms to let."

"A gentleman? Oh, goodness, no. Nothing available." Katie pushed a smaller blue slug back down into the boiling water, then paused to consider what her niece had said. "Wait, what does he look like?"

"He's an older man. A bit thin. Grey hair, beard and glasses."

Sounded like a normal human. "Tell him we have no rooms available."

Nellie stared at the slugs, blue, green and red. "Yech! What are those?"

"They're for Mr. Smzch's dinner. Now go run along and tell the gentleman we have nothing to let."

"Who's Mr. Smzch? I've never seen him."

Considering Mr. Smzch was mostly tentacles that was certainly for the best. "He's in room three. He's shy and keeps to himself mostly." Most of her tenants did...at least in the daylight.

"Why would anyone eat slugs?"

"He has a difficult medical condition," Katie O'Leary replied.

"What about room four. There's no one in there but a six-legged cat."

"The result of a bad birth defect. You should be more charitable, Nellie." Katie hit the large slug again and it fell back into the boiling water. Hopefully not too hard. Smzch didn't like his food battered. Still, the larger ones were hard to cook without hitting them a bit.

"Auntie, the cat smokes a hookah!"

"A filthy foreign habit, I'm sure, but better than cigars. Now run along and tell the gentleman we're full up."

"How about room five?" Nellie asked doggedly. "There's no one in that room."

That wasn't exactly true; there was a very large cockroach in there. Well, not really a cockroach, just something that looked very much like one. Gave Katie the willies every time she saw it, which wasn't often, thank goodness. "I tol' you that room is reserved." Katie gave a final whack to the large blue slug. The blue ones tended to be more feisty.

Nellie threw up her hands and went down the corridor to the door, muttering to herself.

Good girl, Nellie was, but it was too soon for her to know the truth. That took some working up to. Katie herself had found the whole thing difficult to believe when the strange beings first came to her with their proposal: a boarding house for aliens, and not meaning the Irish either.

These were aliens from a lot farther away than the old country. Still they were people—to use the term loosely—who either didn't have a place to stay, or for one reason or another couldn't stay where they were.

Katie could understand that. There were humans in such situations. It had taken her a few weeks to think it out, but then she decided to give it a try. Three years ago it was now. She had no regrets. For one thing, the aliens tended to keep to themselves. There hadn't been a lot of trouble with them, and there was an additional benefit: the aliens paid in gold.

Katie spooned the barely cooked slugs into the large green bowl, adding a sprinkling of the black powder Mr. Smzch liked.

She had five rooms to let and just now they

were all occupied. Mostly by down on their luck aliens. Mr. Marlet, the six-legged cat, went bankrupt in some financial disaster. He tried to explain, but Mrs. O'Leary had no hope of understanding what he was talking about. The cockroach, Mr. Klclktit, was on the run from some situation Katie couldn't quite understand. Not that she wanted to talk too much to a cockroach. She tried to be open-minded, but still bugs as people, well, it didn't seem right.

Mr. Smzch used to be an Emperor of some variety. Talked about a star system revolt. Katie understood revolts at least. Hard not to since the Southern Rebellion hadn't been over five years yet. The Northern States had won, but it had been a very hard fought, nasty war. A lot of people weren't ever the same after that.

Mr. Ovani was in room one. He wasn't on the run from anything; Katie didn't believe he'd ever be afraid of anything. And he wasn't in the least human-like. Mostly sparkling energy. Sometimes he had a shape, most of the time, he didn't.

What her boarders looked like didn't matter. Where they came from, and why they were here, didn't matter either. Weren't none of her business really.

The pan with a half dozen golden spheres began to boil. She put on the special gloves Mr. Ovani gave her and spooned the spheres into a special bowl. Mr. Ovani had told her touching the large, golden marbles could kill her. She was very careful. She poured a silvery liquid over the marbles. That too she must be very, very careful with.

Katie wasn't sure why Mr. Ovani was here. He had a lot of power; she knew that. He'd be shimmering energy one moment, and then he'd have claws, and then tentacles. Very unnerving it was. At least most of the time, when he wasn't just sparkling energy, he wore a black cape. That helped. She didn't necessarily want to see what was under that cloak. If'n it even was a cape. A bit too dark it was for a cloak. Dark, like a sky with no moon or stars.

Also Mr. Ovani didn't speak, not in any real way. He thought at her. She spoke back to him. Too weird to just think her words.

He was very polite, though. Always thanked her for the small extra things she did to try to make him more comfortable. And that time there was the odd, sticky fluid on the carpet, well, he paid handsomely to have it the carpet replaced.

Quiet folk her alien guests were, rarely causing any trouble—except for some of the food they ate. It was well known, though, that foreigners ate different. She knew that going into this.

In truth the aliens were easier than some of the human boarders she had after that most uncivil war. Soldiers with missing limbs she didn't mind. Some of the soldiers, though, had problems in their minds. She understood it was the things they'd seen and done. She, and they, knew they'd likely never be right again. It was very sad, but twice she'd had soldier boarders shoot at nothing. They'd wake from a dream and think the enemy was there. There was a bullet lodged in the wall over her bed.

That had been a bad night. Wasn't long after that, the aliens came to talk to her. Might have been that bullet over her bed that helped set her mind towards the aliens.

Aliens never brought weapons. Mr. Ovani said it wasn't allowed. Good thing. Katie wasn't sure she'd be able to tell an alien weapon if she saw one.

As Katie climbed the back steps to the second floor carrying a tray with the green bowl for Mr. Szmch and the special bowl with Mr. Ovani's spheres, she worried about what to do about Mr. Klckltit, the cockroach. Two months behind in his rent, he was. The only good thing was she wasn't providing board. Mr. Klckltit said he could take care of food on his own.

Katie had a good idea how. She could hear him scurrying about the house after she went to bed and it was rare that she ever found an insect in the house after he moved in. He'd been a boarder for eight months now, but she'd only been paid for six. Two months late was a long time. She'd have to talk to him soon about it.

She knocked on Mr. Smzch's door. He didn't answer it. He rarely did. He only left the bathroom on the afternoons when all her guests gathered downstairs. And then only for a short time. He didn't like leaving the bathroom where he'd paid to have a large bathtub and an overhead watering device installed to keep the room hot and moist. Some sort of invisible energy barrier kept the water from leaking out of the room. Mr. Smzch brought that himself.

The bathroom took up most of the room but there was a small sitting area outside. Katie put down the bowls on the side table and tapped on the inner, bathroom, door.

A grayish-green tentacle opened it.

"Mrs. O'Leary, how nice to see you."

He spoke through a red translating device; all the aliens did. Except Mr. Ovani.

Katie held out the bowl just as one of the blue slugs raised its head. "Oh, dear."

"No, no, Mrs. O'Leary. They are cooked to perfection." A gray-green tentacle wrapped around the bowl and drew it into the overly warm, damp room.

"A good evening to you, sir," Mrs. O'Leary said pleasantly.

Next was Mr. Ovani. She tapped on the door. A clawed hand opened the door. It wasn't attached to anything, just came out of the long cloak. Odd to be wearing a cloak on such a hot day, but she didn't think that mattered to him.

Under the cloak, where a face might be, she sometimes saw stars swirling where his eyes should be. Weren't none of her never-mind. If'n a man had stars for eyes, well truly God blessed him. At least she hoped it was God and not the other guy. Mrs. O'Leary held out the bowl of golden spheres covered with silver sauce.

Thank you kindly, Mrs. O'Leary, he thought at her, taking the bowl. *Looks to be an excellent repast as always.*

He always talked like that, so gentleman-like. Except of course, the words just popped up in her mind. Still maybe better than the grunts and screeches some aliens used when they talked.

"We are getting a bit low on that silver sauce you like. Your grocer needs to drop off more."

I'll tell him.

He closed the door with the clawed hand, which shifted to look like a human hand. Only three fingers, though. Well, didn't matter.

Katie went back downstairs to her large kitchen. Soon she would sit down to her own supper of cold meat pie and fruit.

Nellie was finishing up the wash in the basement. Katie could hear the clacking of the hand wringer. Once the girl was done, they'd eat, and then Nellie would return to her father's house two blocks away. Nellie's mother had died birthing Nellie's youngest brother. The poor man had been left to raise a daughter and two boys on his own.

Katie missed her sister. If she'd lived, Katie was sure she was the one person she could have told about the aliens. No one else, though. Too dangerous for everyone involved.

People in Chicago were as open-minded as any, but there were limits. Octopus-like creatures and giant cockroaches were quite a bit past most people's limits.

They were nearly done eating when the doorbell chimed again.

"Stay, Nellie, and finish your supper. I'll get it," Katie said.

The old oak door with its oval stained glass insert swung open easily. On her wide porch stood someone wearing a long overcoat. As the temperature was over eighty, it was safe to assume he wasn't human.

The sun was setting behind her visitor, so it was hard to see...it...him clearly. As her eyes adjusted to the twilight, she saw, above and below the overcoat, what appeared to be a tall, upright white slug. No arms or legs or eyes. It did have two waving appendages that slipped free from the hat perched on top of its pale oval head. Might be eye stalks. Or antennae. Hard to say with some of the aliens. Well, she wasn't a bigot about her tenants having to have eyes.

It stood there—more like balanced—on a long curve of a tail. Slowly a bit of whitish flesh pinched off the middle and an appendage protruded through the front of the coat holding a flat red disk.

Mrs. O'Leary knew what to do. "My name is

Mrs. Katie O'Leary. I run a boarding house for gentlemen. This is Chicago, in Illinois, in the United States of America." She might have added Earth, but that always felt weird.

That should be enough for his translator to get a fix on the language. She had to go through this every time. A nuisance, but as one of her boarders pointed out, Earth languages weren't well known in the galaxy.

The slug hummed something.

A moment later the red disk translated. "You have rooms to let?"

The voice was flat and uninflected, very alien-sounding. Not that that needed confirming, the gentleman being a large slug and all.

"Well," she began. He seemed like a nice tenant, but even the barn stall was let to Mr. Longger, who looked like a cow, but only on a dark night. She considered the matter. There was the large room the cockroach was in. And he was behind in his rent...

"I might have a room," Mrs. O'Leary said, standing back. "If you would step into my parlor?"

He—she always thought of her tenants as he—undulated towards the room she indicated, past the open pocket doors. He didn't leave a slime trail. That was good.

"Auntie? Who is it?"

Mrs. O'Leary turned down the knob on the gaslight, putting the room into shadows. "I'll be back in a couple of minutes," she told her guest softly and pulled the pocket doors closed.

Nellie was walking down the corridor that ran between the parlors and the front staircase. "Nellie, dear, if you've finished your supper, you probably should be getting on home before it gets too dark."

"Who was at the door?"

"Traveling salesman," Mrs. O'Leary lied without compunction.

The girl looked as though she's might ask something further, but instead she obediently put on her hat. Mrs. O'Leary escorted her to the door and watched as her niece walked down the front steps. Then Katie quietly closed the door and turned to go up the front stairs, her sensible button top shoes clicking firmly on the oak stair treads.

The door to room five was closed. Most of her tenants kept to themselves, except for the first and third Sunday afternoons when they all congregated in her front parlor for tea and cakes.

It was interesting listening to their talk of their lives on other worlds, although there was much she didn't understand. The red disk translating devices had trouble with some of the words. At least she hoped so.

Mrs. O'Leary tapped politely on the door. There was a scittering, scuttling sound. "Come in, Mrs. O'Leary."

Katie hesitantly opened the door; she always

felt uncomfortable around the large insect.Mr. Klclktit was perched on his many legs in the middle of the Turkish carpet, almost blending into the complex design with his iridescent shell. The red disk communicator sat on top of his head.

"If you have come for the rent, I'm afraid that my...family...has not contacted me lately. I will pay you all I owe. I swear it!" The disk throbbed slightly. The actual speech sounds came from inside the hard shell. Kinda like a hard file on metal. Not pleasant.

"I believe you, Mr. Klckltit." Katie folded her hands in front of her long, dark blue dress. "But I was wondering if you really needed all this room?"

The cockroach—she could only think of him as that—settled back on his rear four legs. He was about the size of a small cat and had a dozen legs.

"What do you mean?"

"I have another...guest...asking for a room."

"One of us, I presume?"

"I only rent to...well, I don't rent to humans." It was hard to say who, or what, she rented to other than they weren't human.

"Hmmm," the cockroach considered the matter. "The attic?" he offered.

"I could have a room made up there," Mrs. O'Leary offered, wondering why she hadn't thought of that before.

"That won't be necessary," the cockroach said politely. "I really don't use the bed, you know."

"Will it take you long to pack?" she asked.

The cockroach tittered, which was quite unnerving. "I don't have much to pack. I can be gone within a few minutes."

"That would be properly nice of you." She wished she didn't feel so uncomfortable around him.

"Any part of the attic you prefer that I use?" the cockroach asked.

"No, take the whole attic." It was the least she could do. "Obviously, your rent will be much reduced."

"I should think so."

"Well, thank you again," Mrs. O'Leary said formally, closing the door as she left.

She went back down the stairs and pulled open the pocket door. The upper body of the alien swiveled towards her. The eye stalks, she was pretty sure that was what they were, turned in her direction. The alien had shed his overcoat and hat. He was, indeed, a large, pale white slug with a vague circle for a mouth, and a slender tail that he balanced on.

"I have a room," she announced. "I wish to clean it a bit, but if you wait here, it won't take me long. As for costs, for long-term tenants— meaning a month or more—rent is a dollar fifty per week. If you are going to be here only a short time," she added, "the cost is two dollars a week."

She didn't like short-term boarders, but sometimes it happened. She couldn't afford to be overly choosy.

"I doubt if the room needs cleaning."

It really didn't, but still she had a reputation to consider. "If it is acceptable to you, I'll do a thorough cleaning tomorrow." Katie was a bit tired.

"That will be fine." He paused a moment, then continued. "I'm not sure how long I will be staying," the slug said. "Maybe a week, maybe a couple of months."

Mrs. O'Leary was used to that as well. "Well, then I have to charge you the short term rent. Board is seventy-five cents per week, if'n my grocer has what you need. Otherwise your grocer has to supply it."

"I've brought my own food," the tall slug said.

"If it's alive, it'll have to stay in the barn," Mrs. O'Leary said firmly.

"No, it's liquid."

"I like my boarders to pay a week in advance."

"I don't have any of the local currency, but I was told that you accept gold."

"I prefer it," Mrs. O'Leary said honestly.

An appendage grew out of the slug. It twisted to reach into himself. That was a little disconcerting, but she'd seen odder things.

"This is the smallest I have. It should cover a month I would think." The slug held out a small gold coin.

Mrs. O'Leary knew the coin, once it was melted down, would cover more like six or seven month's rent. That was a major benefit to renting to aliens, most of the time they overpaid. It wasn't like she could give change.

She took the coin and tucked into the pocket of her simple blue dress. "I'll show you to your room. How do you wish to be addressed?" She had learned to ask the question that way. Some alien cultures had no idea what a name was, but they all seemed to understand the idea of being addressed. Or maybe it was just the universal translator understood that better.

"Carminet."

Katie led the way to the front staircase, the one the boarders used. It was wide oak with nicely carved ornate newel posts. All the boarding rooms were on the second floor.

Her own bedroom was on the first floor, just off the back parlor. She preferred her boarders stayed upstairs and she stayed downstairs. Except when she bought them their food. And the twice a month gatherings in the front parlor.

The slug had a little difficulty with the steps, but he managed. "Do you have any *clorits* staying here?" he asked.

Mrs. O'Leary shook her head. "I have no one named Clorits here."

"*Clorits* are a species," the slug corrected her. "Quite common in the galaxy."

"I don't know anything about what's common in the galaxy," Katie replied quite honestly. "All my tenants are respectable folk, though, I'll tell you that."

She turned around to face the slug, to make her point clear and saw the yellow pulsating circle beneath the eye stalks. "Humor signal," the translator explained.

Hmmph, so he found that amusing. Well, her boarders were quiet and respectable while they were at her house. She wouldn't put up with them if they weren't.

The yellow pulsating ebbed as they got to the top step. "*Clorits* have a dozen legs and a *curentiz* covering," the slug explained further.

Katie wished the universal translators would do a better job with proper nouns. She had no idea what a *curentiz* covering was. "If'n a creature has a dozen legs, then that's what God gave him," she stated bluntly. "I don't allow no bigotry here." She might not like the cockroach, but she would certainly defend any creature's right to have as many legs as it needed—or as was given—by God.

"I understand and agree," the slug said soothingly. "Do your tenants ever get together?" he added. "Ever talk together, all the guests are in one place?"

"Yes," Mrs. O'Leary said, hoping the slug— Mr. Carminet—was going to be reasonable. She'd had trouble between two of her tenants once.

Very messy. Had to throw the carpet out. "First and third Sunday afternoons we meet in the front parlor. I serve tea to those who like it and can drink it." Only the cat, Mr. Marlet, and the cow, Mr. Longger, drank it, though. The cat drank it through his pipe, which seemed odd, but she had always served tea to her guests on the first and third Sundays before she had started taking in aliens, so it didn't seem right to stop just because they were different.

"All your guests meet on these days?" the slug asked.

"And sometimes aliens from other … places … join us."

"When will the gathering next occur?" Mr. Carminet asked.

"Well, today is the third Wednesday, so four more days." She opened the door to room five. "Solar cycles," she amended to help him understand.

Mr. Carminet glided partway into the room and paused. "So very…quaint," he offered.

Mrs. O'Leary wasn't sure how to take that. "Thank you," she said, deciding it was a compliment. "Rooms are cleaned every other day, with dusting, sweeping and a change of linens on Saturday. If you prefer a different schedule, let me know."

"That's fine," Mr. Carminet said politely. "I am very much looking forward to meeting your other guests."

"I won't abide any trouble here," she warned him again.

"No trouble at all," the slug agreed quietly.

The next four days passed without incident. Katie thought about asking Mr. Klckltit about his back rent, but after sending him to the attic, it seemed rude. Mr. Klckltit wouldn't be the first of her tenants who fell behind in paying her— even before she started taking in aliens. Next month, though, she'd have to get firm with him.

Sunday afternoon her "gentlemen," as she preferred to call them, began gathering in her front parlor. The drapes, which were seldom open, where drawn particularly close. The gas lamps were turned up, but not too high. Katie wasn't always sure she liked to see her guests too closely herself.

The cow-like gentleman, Mr. Longger, came in from the barn. He was first to arrive. Tracked in a bit of mud, he did. Hard to wipe hooves off. He apologized profusely, but Mrs. O'Leary was used to his tracking a bit of dirt in on these gatherings. Told him it was no never-mind.

Those that could settled in chairs and those that couldn't stood or sat about the wide rug. Mr. Smzch oozed over to a leather sheet she put out for him. Saved the carpet from the damp. He was wearing a wrap to keep the hot moisture in.

By the time the tea was ready, Mr. Klckltit still hadn't arrived and the new boarder, Mr. Carminet, was also missing. Maybe she should go to the attic and tell Mr. Klckltit he was still welcome at the Sunday gathering. He might be feeling left out up there in the attic. As soon as the tea was poured, she'd do that.

Mr. Smzch liked having tea in a large mug. He never drank any, but sometimes he dangled the tip of a tentacle in it. Mr. Marlet, the six-legged cat, held out his pipe. She obligingly poured it full of English Breakfast tea. He liked English Breakfast best. Mr. Longger took his tea in a bowl. He lapped it up.

Among themselves, the aliens didn't always use a universal translator. At least two languages were being spoken, or so Katie thought, because there were both trilling sounds and grunts. Mr. Ovani didn't speak, but she had the feeling he was talking with the others just the same. Sometimes, she even felt a little of it. She'd get a vision of long fleets of ships that sailed between the stars, beautiful ships that shifted and changed like he did. Shifting and altering with perception and reality—as though these concepts were not immutable.

Well, that came close to giving her the vapors, it did, so she ignored that, and continued to sit with her guests and be a good hostess.

In the hallway, outside the parlor, there was the sound of many feet clicking on the hardwood floor. Mr. Klckltit skittered in.

"I'm glad you could join us," Mrs. O'Leary said formally. "Would you like some tea?" He never did, but it was only proper to offer it.

"No, thank you," he said.

The other aliens shifted around a bit. Katie got the feeling they didn't like him much.

"There is a new guest," she said taking her seat again. "I thought for sure he'd join us. He asked particularly about meeting everyone."

That seemed to get their attention.

"Who?" several of them asked through their translators.

"A Mr. Carminet," Mrs. O'Leary said. "Tall and pale."

"Carminet?" Mr. Longger asked. "What species is he?"

"I'm not sure," Mrs. O'Leary said.

"Bounty hunter," the slug answered, standing by the door. He wasn't wearing the overcoat anymore and a pinched off bit of white flesh held what looked like a weapon.

"I don't allow..." Mrs. O'Leary began sternly, but was interrupted by a harsh humming sound.

Mr. Klckltit became a pile of dust.

The other aliens did not seem terribly upset.

"Well done," Mr. Smzch said, waving several of his tentacles.

The slug slid into the room. He performed an elaborate head bobbing towards Mr. Smzch. "Your *ittilig* majesty." He turned towards Mr. Ovani and curved his long body in half. "Most honored, sir."

The long cape Mr. Ovani wore billowed outward a little. Mrs. O'Leary thought she could see through him, to somewhere far away where a star was being born. She shivered.

"His *wanit* polluted the *esost*. Thank you for disposing of him," Mr. Marlet raised his hookah to the slug and then to Mr. Ovani.

Mrs. O'Leary didn't know what a *"wanit"* or *"esost"* was, and wasn't sure she wanted to.

Mr. Ovani drew his cloak more fully around his...body...as he turned towards Mrs. O'Leary. *I let the bounty hunters know Klckltit was here. He is wanted through most of the known galaxies for genocide.*

Mrs. O'Leary had the feeling that if Mr. Ovani had chosen to, he could have easily disposed of Mr. Klckltit. Maybe even a star system.

He—and his egg mates—knowingly consumed an entire species, Mr. Ovani added.

"Oh," Mrs. O'Leary said.

His egg mates have been destroyed. It was Klckltit's time.

A pouch appeared on the slug's side. He put the weapon he'd been holding in it and pulled a wand-type object out. Gliding over to the remains of Mr. Klckltit, he waved the wand over the pile of dust, sucking it up. "Plenty of evidence to claim the reward."

Mrs. O'Leary immediately thought of how useful such a device would be to clean carpets.

W. F. Halsey   26

Maybe she could talk to one of the aliens about it later.

"No trouble, I trust, Mrs. O'Leary?" the slug asked politely.

Well, it wasn't as though Mr. Klckltit had been one of her favorite tenants. And if Mr. Ovani approved...well, it must be right.

"No, problem, Mr. Carminet. I take it you won't be staying much longer."

"Just till nightfall."

"If you'd like a refund?" After all, he had just stayed a few days.

The soft yellow glowed beneath his eye stalks. "No, thank you, Mrs. O'Leary. Please keep it to compensate you for your kindness."

The aliens were like that mostly. Nice people.

And now she had another room to let...but maybe not to any more cockroaches.

Illusions

Katie spread the slightly damp tea leaves across the imported Turkish carpet. The rug was expensive with fine dark red colors in an intricate design. Some might wonder how she could afford such a luxury with such a small boarding house, but since the carpet was in the back parlor, few ever saw it. And it wasn't the oddest aspect of the house, for a fact.

Mrs. O'Leary could afford the high priced carpet because her boarders mostly paid in ornamental gold coins. On Earth the value of the coins was rather a bit higher than the price for room and board. Gold, however, wasn't as rare in some parts of the galaxy as it was on Earth.

She pushed the tea leaves around the wool carpet with her large broom, picking up bits of dust. She'd learned this trick from her mother who had also had a lovely Turkish rug. It wasn't quite a nice as this one, and besides that one had gone to her brother who lived three streets over.

Katie didn't begrudge him the lovely carpet, especially now that she had her own.

She hummed an old Irish tune as she finished sweeping the tea leaves across the carpet. A fine

autumn day it was and her boarding house was
full again. The small room that Mr. Klclktit had
before he moved to the attic, the one the bounty
hunter lived in for just three days, was now
occupied by a most unusual boarder. And given
what her usual clientele was like, that was
saying something. The odd part was the reason
he was unusual: he looked human.

The gentleman had arrived just the day
before. She'd almost sent him away 'til she saw
the universal translator pinned to the lapel of his
coat. Universal translators were bright red. Hard
to miss it and humans didn't wear them.

Although there were times when they could
be handy for humans. Like when Mr. Hawkins,
at the butcher's shop, started talking with that
broad Scottish accent. Half the time Katie had to
just hope she got what she ordered. Sometimes
she didn't.

This gentleman looked like a man in his mid-
thirties. Said his name was Smith. Odd name for
an alien, for sure.

About average height, brown hair. Seemed a
little fuzzy around the edges, but overall quite
human. His dress had seemed odd at first, plaid
pants and a strongly checked jacket. She might
have seen that wrong, though, because when she
looked again, his suit was a subdued brown.

With luck this gentleman would be a more
long term guest. She preferred stability; guests
who stayed for months, or even years. Many of

her boarders did.

Mr. Longger, Mr. Marlet, and Mr. Ovani had all been with her almost from the beginning. Mr. Szmch had joined the household the following year. She had had a few short term guests before Mr. Szmch had arrived.

Katie preferred long term guests, always had. Most any rooming house did. But now that she took in aliens, it was even more the case. Humans varied a bit, but nothing like the aliens.

They were all God's people, she reminded herself. Aliens were probably not all that different from, say, a Chinaman.

That might be true of some, like Mr. Marlet, the six-legged cat. Other than smoking a hookah, and liking barely cooked meat, he wasn't that unusual. Well, besides being a cat and having six legs.

No point in trying to convince herself the aliens weren't more than a bit odd. Still the pay was good. It just took more time getting used to each new alien species. They had some real peculiarities. To be sure, humans did as well, but not so much.

Katie swept the tea leaves, now encrusted with dust, into a dust pan. Walking to the kitchen she noticed it was getting time to cook Mr. Szmch's slugs.

She stopped suddenly in the middle of the kitchen, puzzled. What did Mr. Smith eat? And how had she forgotten to ask him?

She'd been so surprised to see a human-
looking alien, the first thing she did was tell him
Mr. Ovani said there were no species in the
galaxies that looked like humans. Mr. Smith
smiled so nicely and said the Ovani were not
always correct.

Mrs. O'Leary had a bit of trouble believing
that. Mr. Ovani seemed to know everything.
Still, all beings could make mistakes; Mr. Ovani
wasn't God after all.

Katie crossed herself and said a quick Hail
Mary. Maybe later tonight she'd go to Mass. It
had been a couple of days since she'd been to
church. She did so enjoy sitting in the pews at
St. Mary's listening to Father O'Malley's Latin.
Such a nice voice he had.

Well, no point in dawdling around. She'd have
to go upstairs now and ask Mr. Smith what he
ate. So odd of her to forget that. Odd, too, that
Mr. Smith had asked her most particular like not
to tell the Ovani he was staying at her house.

Katie had agreed somewhat hesitantly. She
didn't like keeping secrets from Mr. Ovani. Still,
if a boarder wanted privacy that was his right.
So long as there wasn't any trouble with the law,
privacy wasn't a problem. And realistically all
her guests were outside the law, way outside.

Besides, Mr. Ovani was working on
something that demanded his complete
attention. He didn't even want food brought for
the next few days. Not that Mr. Ovani ate every

day; he told her when he wanted her to prepare a meal for him. If'n you could call metals balls with a silver sauce a meal.

Tapping on Mr. Smith's door, Katie waited for his response.

"Mrs. O'Leary?" the translator in the room responded.

"I have a few more questions, if you don't mind." The translator relayed that in a series of grunts and snaps which apparently was Mr. Smith's native language.

The door opened. Mr. Smith stood there properly dressed in his brown tweed suit. He seemed older than she remembered. He seemed more like a man in his fifties now. Maybe she wasn't remembering right what he looked like before.

His eyes though were still a lovely shade of brown. That she remembered right. Still a little fuzzy around the edges, like he was somehow not quite complete. Well, that wasn't important.

Mrs. O'Leary stepped into the room. The bed didn't look slept in. Or maybe Mr. Smith just remade the bed exactly like she did. Didn't matter.

Her guests did their own housekeeping most days. Twice a week, Katie changed linens and swept and dusted each room. In between, the guests tended their rooms themselves. If it needed tending. Octopus like creatures and whatever Mr. Ovani was, well, they didn't make much mess. Or sleep in beds. Maybe Mr. Smith, for all that he looked human, didn't sleep in a bed either.

"How can I help you?" Mr. Smith stood very still, unnatural-like, as though he wasn't sure quite how to stand or move.

"I forgot to ask if you wanted board?"

"Why would I want wood?"

A common mistake. Katie needed to remember the translator could be quite literal and couldn't tell the difference between board, as in wood, and board as in food. "Board, in a rooming house like this, means providing food. For some of my guests, I provide, or sometimes just cook, meals for them. I just do supper really. All guests are on their own for breakfast and lunch."

Mr. Smith tilted his head a little. Or maybe the area around his head just got fuzzier. "Are you asking me what do I eat?"

"Well, more specifically I'm asking if you require me to provide you with some sort of supper, or to prepare your supper?"

"What do humans eat for this supper occasion?"

"Usually some sort of meat and potatoes, or maybe cabbage. In the summer and fall, I can offer some vegetables or fresh fruit."

The translator issued another series of grunts and some noises that weren't quite snapping sounds, but more like wheezes.

"Meat? You mean a dead carcass?"

Said that way, it didn't sound all that appetizing. Mrs. O'Leary decided to change tactics. "Mr. Szmch has his meat delivered once a week. It is alive when it is delivered. He eats...um, slugs. Barely cooked. If you have a grocer who can deliver food that you like, that's fine. He has to come after dark. All deliveries, of any type, have to be made after dark."

"Yes, anyone approaching this planet has to come at the dark phase of that section of the planet. That is known."

They were wandering off the topic. "So, do you need me to provide food for you?"

Mr. Smith smiled most engagingly. "I will try a human meal tomorrow night. Whatever would be appropriate for a human to eat."

"I was planning on making corned beef and cabbage for myself for dinner tomorrow with fresh picked green beans from Mrs. Hanover's garden and an apple pie."

The translator hesitated over a few of those words. Katie was sure exactly what Mr. Smith heard. He seemed a bit puzzled, but nodded after a moment. "Whatever a human would eat, I will try."

"Do you need anything for supper tonight?"

"No, thank you, Mrs. O'Leary. I will wait until tomorrow to try your human food."

Very pleasant was Mr. Smith.

Katie went back down the front stair case. Part way down, she stumbled, her heel catching on the stair. She started to plummet forward. Panic spiked for a moment, then she caught hold of the handrail. For a moment she had seen herself, battered and crumpled at the bottom of the stairs. She could have been killed. Her heart pounded wildly.

She finished descended the steps, carefully holding the wide oak handrail. She couldn't think of the last time she had been so careless. Slowly, her heart resumed a more normal rhythm

Putting the tea kettle on the still warm stove, she decided a nice cup of tea would help settle her nerves. She had a little leftover chicken in the icebox. Make a nice bit of soup for tonight's supper.

After she got Mr. Szmch's supper up to him. She pulled out a half dozen smallish pieces of wood from the storage box next to the stove. She never kept much there. Wouldn't be safe. She wouldn't need much wood tonight. No need to go to the wood box on the porch. She added a second cast iron pot of water on the stove for Mr. Szmch's slugs. She never used that pot for anything else. However open-minded she might be about aliens and their ways, she wasn't cooking her dinner in any pan what had had slugs in it.

Putting the wood into the cast iron fire box,

she wrapped a shawl around her shoulders and went through the back yard to the small two stall barn to get Mr. Szmch's slugs.

Mr. Longger, who looked rather like a cow with a too round head and no udders, looked up as she entered the barn.

"Good evening, Mrs. O'Leary." Mr. Longger's native language wasn't too different from a cow's, a sort of mooing with some high-pitched accents. The red translator hung around his neck like a bell.

"Good evening, Mr. Longger. How has your day been?"

"Boring, as always. But I have a new immersion simulator arriving tomorrow. It even has smell encoded. Very nice that will be."

Mrs. O'Leary had no idea what he was referring to, but so long as it didn't create a problem, it didn't matter. She knew Mr. Longger sometimes he stuck his head into a box set at the end of his stall. Judging by his mooing sounds, he liked it very much. Maybe that was what the simulation thing was.

"Are you planning on going out again tonight?" she asked as she picked up a box of slugs from the upper shelf of the ice box. The slugs couldn't be kept too close to the ice. That killed them and Mr. Szmch wanted them barely boiled, so they had to start out fresh, meaning alive.

"Yes. I'll be more careful this time. There is a

nice bit of open land not too far from here. I'd like to wander around it a bit."

"Getting to be less and less pasture around here, but still a little. Just don't talk back if anyone tries to bring you back here. And definitely don't fight them! Everyone around here knows you belong in this barn, so if they try to lead you back, you just come along. No trouble."

"That human was very rude, tugging at me like that. Besides, no human will be expecting me late at night."

"You butted him rather hard. And I told you not to go out in the daylight unless I was with you."

"I don't like to inconvenience you."

"Well, we've made it part of your room and board agreement that we go to the pasture together once a week."

"I like being out in the sun light. I like the taste of that fresh...green...stuff."

Translator didn't quite get the word grass right, or maybe Mr. Longger didn't. Either way, Mrs. O'Leary understood.

"Well, just be careful and I'll check on you in the morning." When Katie got back in the kitchen the teakettle was good and hot and the water was just beginning to boil in Mr. Szmch's cast iron pot.

She added a big pinch of the seasoning Mr. Szmch had sent from wherever he came from to the pot and opened the odd shaped box. Taking out three slugs: one blue, one green and a small red one, she dropped them into the boiling water. The red ones weren't too common she'd been told. Not all boxes had red ones in it.

It made no never mind to her. The only real problem was all boxes had blue slugs and they were the biggest and the most feisty. This one wasn't an exception. She had to whack it several times to keep it from getting out of the pot. Took only a few moments and they were done the way Mr. Szmch liked them. She spooned the slugs into a bowl and sprinkled on some of the black powder that looked like pepper, but definitely wasn't.

For some odd reason she thought she'd like to feel how the dish felt with all the seasonings and the boiling water and the slugs. She put her fingers into the bowl. And yelped.

What the Hell! She crossed herself; she'd say the rosary later in penance for swearing.

Why would she do something like that?

"Hot was it?"

Mr. Smith was standing across the kitchen by the sink.

"Not just hot. Those spices, whatever they are, burn worse."

"Hmmm, I suspect they are heat activated."

Mrs. O'Leary ran her fingers under the cold water. Stupid idea. Why would she ever think to do a thing like that?

She needed to get Mr. Szmch his dinner
before it got cold. Shaking the water off her
fingers, she picked up the bowl and went
upstairs by the back staircase, the one that led
off the kitchen to the second floor. "We should
talk when I'm done, Mr. Smith."

"At your disposal," he grunted. Well, he
grunted; the translator had a very pleasant
voice.

'At your disposal'? My wasn't he the
gentleman, Mrs. O'Leary thought as she tapped
on the outer door of Mr. Szmch's room.

"Come in."

Mrs. O'Leary opened the outer door, and
tapped again on the inner one before opening it
and putting the bowl through. It was always a
bit odd, pushing the bowl through the force field.
Like pushing through a thick bit of mush, but
she was used to it.

Going back down the stairs, she saw Mr.
Smith was still in the kitchen.

"Mr. Smith, I am at fault because I didn't
fully explain the rules here. You startled me
being so human-like. One of the main rules is the
guests remain upstairs during the day. I know
you look mostly like a human, so going outside
the house might be allowed, particularly at
twilight, or at night. However, the downstairs is
where I live. As you like your privacy, so do I."

"How am I not completely like a human?"

"Well, you're a bit fuzzy around the edges to

start with. Most people might not notice, but still best not to be out in bright sunlight." Mrs. O'Leary took the leftover chicken leg out of the ice box and started to cut the meat off the bone. "Now, I used to have gathering times every other Sunday when all my guests who want to are invited downstairs for refreshments. Because you people don't get out much, I've decided to make it every Sunday afternoon between one p.m. and four p.m. Any of my guests can gather in the front parlor. You are most welcome to join your fellow guests at that time."

Mrs. O'Leary yelped again. She'd cut herself. "Mary and Joseph, how clumsy I'm getting." It wasn't bad, but she was back at the sink again running water over her finger.

She had gauze in the pantry. She used the knife to cut a strip and wrapped her finger.

Mr. Smith continued to stand in the kitchen watching her. "What is a son-day? Do you have children?"

Mrs. O'Leary sighed. This is why she did not like short term guests. Took so long to get language and customs worked out.

"Today is Thursday – Thor's Day my granny used to remind us. Never sure just how good a Christian she was. Never mind. The next solar cycle will be Friday, then Saturday, and then Sunday. So basically the third solar cycle from now, in the afternoon, everyone who wishes it, will come to the front parlor." She was tempted to explain the reasons for the names of the other days of the week, but thought better of it. No sense in confusing Mr. Smith further.

Mr. Ovani had taught her how to explain days. It seemed very straight-forward to her: there were days and there were nights. All this solar cycle nonsense didn't make sense to her, but it did to her guests. That's what mattered.

"Thank you for explaining. I might join you."

Mrs. O'Leary took a couple of carrots and an onion from the pantry. She had harvested them that morning. She didn't have the time, or really the space, for a large garden, but she did grow herbs and tomatoes, carrots and onions. Vegetables that took little work or attention.

She looked up and Mr. Smith was still standing there. "Good evening," she said firmly.

Mr. Smith bowed slightly and left, going up the back staircase. His bowing was quite nice, elegant actually, but the back staircase was her territory. Her guests used the wide front staircase. She used the front staircase as well sometimes; her guests, however, were not supposed to use the back staircase. If'n for no other reason than it was quite narrow.

She sighed. Something else she'd have to explain to Mr. Smith.

Sunday was bright and sunny. That was good. Harder for her neighbors to see into the dimly lit front parlor. Not that they had that much of a chance of that, the drapes being pulled so close.

Mrs. O'Leary would have pinned them, but that would have ruined the décor she was rather proud of.

Both the front and back parlors were a mix of heavy Victorian furniture, elaborately carved, with its long coverings on the chairs and the sofas, so no one could see, or comment, on a leg, even of a chair, with an additional touch of Neoclassical, mostly around the fireplace. The mantel was fluted as were the bookcases that flanked the large stone fireplace.

Mrs. O'Leary set out the tea pot and several cups. Most of which would never be used, but it seemed polite to pretend they might be.

Mrs. O'Leary was moving more carefully. She had been tremendously clumsy lately. Two more of her fingers had gauze around them, and her knee was scraped when she fell down the stairs on the porch. It was only three steps, but still she ached rather a bit from the awkward fall. And her clumsiness seemed contagious; Nellie had three accidents in the past three days. Cut herself on a piece of broken glass, tripped and fell over the carpet in the hallway and burned herself picking up a hot pot. None of the injuries were serious, but painful enough.

Just as the clock chimed one, Mr. Szmch slithered down the staircase, gliding over the oilcloth she laid down. He was, as usual, wrapped in an additional oil cloth to keep the warm moisture he needed close to his body. He also had a pan of hot water set under the cloth.

Mr. Longger clattered in from the barn. Hopefully the neighbors didn't notice the cow coming into the house.

One neighbor had once. Mrs. O'Leary had convinced her the cow had just come close to the porch in grazing. Mrs. O'Leary wasn't sure the old biddy believed that, but it was certainly more reasonable than a cow coming in a house.

Mr. Longger was the only one of her guests who actually drank the tea from anything like a cup; he drank it from a bowl, but close enough. He didn't like his tea strong or very hot so she always made his tea special for him.

Mr. Marlet's six-legs easily managed the staircase around the oilcloth. Like any feline, he did not like getting his paws wet, and Mr. Szmch did leave a damp trail behind him.

"Mr. Ovani won't be joining us," Mr. Marlet announced. "I stopped by his room to remind him, but he is very involved."

Mrs. O'Leary wanted to ask in what, but that would have been intruding. Mr. Ovani was entitled to his privacy as well.

Katie poured out tea for those guests that took it in such ways as they did. She turned off her translator. Such a babble of voices and translations, it was hard to keep up with what they were saying. Some of the guests had there translators set for human so she did get some idea of the conversations. Mostly gossip. What was happening back home; who was in power and who wasn't. Certainly none of her concern.

Also a bit about Cats. They talked about Cats with a capital C. Apparently there was a Cat empire. At least that was how the translator handled the words. The heir to the throne was apparently a bit of a handful. Very young and imperious.

Just like her neighbors or her brother-in-law talking about the kids or their relatives, or politics. Interesting that the species so different had such similar discussions.

Mr. Szmch dangled one of his tentacles in his tea; Mr. Marlet blew tea flavored bubbles in his hookah. The conversation flow moved back and forth.

"Oh, I have a new guest, a new boarder," Mrs. O'Leary cut into their talk.

They turned to look at her. "Who?" came from a variety of translators. Worry in most of the tones. Interesting that the translators could pick up on tone sometimes.

"A gentlemen who looks very human," she replied. "Mr. Ovani said there were no species that looked like us, but Mr. Smith definitely does look human."

The aliens exchanged looks, at least those that had anything like eyes did.

"The Ovani are usually correct," Mr. Longger commented. "And I've never seen any species that looked like a human."

There seemed general agreement on this.

"Well, Mr. Smith prefers his privacy," Mrs. O'Leary said. "So I doubt he'll be here. He told me not to tell Mr. Ovani about his arrival."

"If you want my opinion, I would straight away tell the Ovani about this...being." Mr. Szmch splashed his tentacle about in the wide cup. "Who knows what sort of being this creature could be?"

Coming from an octopus like thing, that could have been rather funny, but Mrs. O'Leary was not inclined to laugh. She wondered if Mr. Szmch was right. 'Tis true any person had a right to privacy, but sometimes Mr. Smith made her a bit nervous. Seemed to be around too much when the small accidents happened. Maybe he was just bad luck?

There were folk tales back in Ireland about creatures who brought bad luck. She never believed in the old tales, but maybe there was some truth in them.

"Tell the Ovani," Mr. Marlet recommended.

Then the conversation turned to other matters and Mrs. O'Leary didn't listen to the details. She refilled Mr. Marlet's hookah and added just a bit of hot tea to Mr. Szmch's pot of hot water. He's told her the steam from the tea added a little different flavor to the moisture under the oil cloth. Mr. Longger had finished his bowl of tea and Mrs. O'Leary poured him another one. Mr. Longger had also nibbled on a

small cake, making rather a mess, but Mrs.
O'Leary would sweep the floor later. There was
no expensive carpet in this room.

Promptly at four p.m. her remaining guests
departed. Mr. Szmch had already left. He
usually stayed less than an hour. He simply
couldn't keep enough moisture under the
oilcloth.

Mr. Smith had never shown up. That hadn't
surprised Mrs. O'Leary.

Monday was wash day. On Sunday evening
Mrs. O'Leary gathered the sheets, pillow cases
and towels from her guests' rooms. Except Mr.
Ovani. She might pretend Mr. Marlet slept in his
bed, and she even changed the sheets in the
outer room where Mr. Szmch stayed, but it was
ridiculous to pretend Mr. Ovani had any use for
a bed. And besides, she didn't want to bother
him.

Mr. Smith, as pleasant as he usually was,
offered to carry the sheets down to the basement
where the washing tub was.

Nellie arrived before dawn. They would need
to get two batches of wash done before she left
for school. After school, Nellie would be back to
help with another batch of washing.

Nellie had a large pan of water boiling on the
stove. The first set of washing was in the large
metal tub. Katie had half-filled the tub with cold
water from the basement tap. One of the hardest
jobs on wash day was carrying the hot water

from the kitchen down the back staircase to the laundry tub in the basement.

Mrs. O'Leary was considering the extravagance of the stove in the basement to make wash day easier. Wouldn't have to be as fancy as the stove in the kitchen. One burner with a fire box below is all that would be needed.

Mr. Smith was standing a little back from the stove. As often as Mrs. O'Leary had told him the downstairs was her private area, he wouldn't listen. She could have gotten firmer, but he was both helpful and nice.

Nellie reached for the large pot of boiling water. Mrs. O'Leary could see something was wrong. Nellie was reaching for one edge of the pot not the handle, and she had no pot holder on her hand! She would spill the boiling water all over herself!

"Nellie, stop! Stop!"

A low throated noise made Mrs. O'Leary turn to Mr. Smith. And she saw something very different. There was a shimmering of someone – something – she had called Mr. Smith, but what was clearer, was the ugly, dark green troll like being. The reality of Mr. Smith. His orange eyes, all four of them, glowed. His tall ears were tufted. No, not a bit human.

"Nellie! Don't touch that pot!"

The girl put her hand down, not even realizing what she had almost done. She looked at her aunt, puzzled. "What's the matter?"

As Mrs. O'Leary continued to stare at Mr. Smith, the troll vanished and the middle-aged man was back again. Still a little fuzzy around the edges. She should have realized it was an illusion. He turned his now brown, and only two of them, eyes towards her. "Is there a problem, Mrs. O'Leary?"

"Nellie, you go home, girl. Go home now."

"But auntie, we haven't started the wash!"

"Wash will be here tomorrow. Don't talk back! Get home now and fix your father a nice breakfast. I'll see you tomorrow."

Nellie looked back and forth between her aunt and Mr. Smith and shrugged. "Want me to take the pot to the sink? I know it's heavy for you."

"Sweet child, you are not to touch that pot. You just go home."

The tone of Katie's voice convinced her and with one long backward glance, she slipped out the back door.

"Mrs. O'Leary," Mr. Smith began mildly. "You seem rather agitated. I know you've said you don't want me in your private spaces, but I just brought down the basket of laundry."

Katie's hand closed on the heavy rolling pin by the stove. She'd been making biscuits before Nellie arrived. No sense to let a warm stove go to waste.

"I saw what you really are." The rolling pin came out from behind her back. "I saw what you tried to make my niece do. Spill that boiling water all over herself."

"Whatever are you talking about? I couldn't do that."

"You are a short, hairy troll. Green. With four eyes. Orange eyes. You can make people see things that aren't true. All those times I cut myself. I couldn't understand how that kept happening when the knife was nowhere near my fingers. You made me believe that. As you are trying to make me believe you look like a human right now."

Actually now that she knew the truth, she could see the human form was shadowy; stare at it closely and you could almost see through him. Look down and stare hard and you could see the nasty little creature that he really was.

"Get out, you perverted Hell-spawned bastard!" Katie almost never swore but she had no regrets about this. "You like to see people in pain! And drop your little illusion. I can see right through it now."

Mr. Smith, or whoever he was, backed towards the door. "I was careful. No one ever got hurt much. A bit of blood, a bruise of two. Nothing really bad."

Mrs. O'Leary advanced on him, tapping the heavy wooden rolling pin in her hand. "I'll bruise you! Maybe I'll see what color your blood is! That boiling water would have scarred my niece. She would have been in tremendous pain!"

Mr. Smith scampered backwards towards the

door.

"Get your sorry ass out of this house! You wait in the barn until dark and then you leave! And if I see anything of you again, I swear, you will be the one who does the bleeding. And if Mr. Longger so much as has a hang nail, I will be discussing you with Mr. Ovani."

"Please, don't tell the Ovani! I'll leave quietly."

"You bet your heathen ass you will!"

The illusion had completely dropped and the hairy green troll ducked to go through the short door she had set in the much larger door back door. Swinging closed, it hit him in the back of the head as he went out.

You are correct, he feeds off the pain. The thought formed in Mrs. O'Leary's mind.

She turned and saw Mr. Ovani in the doorway to the kitchen. Hard to say he was in the doorway since he was mostly swirling colors.

"You knew he was here?"

Not until just now. Your anger broke into...into my thoughts.

"Well, the bastard is gone." Mrs. O'Leary reminded herself to moderate her language. "He would have hurt my niece. Made her think her hand was protected and she was reaching for the handle of the pot." The thought of what could have happened made her shiver with fear. Maybe Nellie should just stay home; maybe it would be safer for her.

When did the grufun arrive?

It took Mrs. O'Leary a moment to realize Mr. Ovani was referring to Mr. Smith.

"The bastard...I'm sorry for my language. I'm still upset." She was, indeed, still shivering with fear and with the horror of what almost happened. "He arrived four days ago."

You usually tell me when you have a new guest. The thought was gentle, but with a touch of reproach.

"You were very involved with whatever it was you are doing." Mrs. O'Leary began and realized she wasn't being fair putting all the blame on him. "And Mr. Smith asked me not to tell you he was here."

I know I can seem a bit distant.

Mrs. O'Leary choked down a half hysterical laugh. A bit distant? This coming from a being who was mostly swirling colors. Just now a set of claws was reaching out, changing to something that, well, there wasn't a word for it. Not a human word at least.

However, I would appreciate it if you would tell me about any new guest. The thought curled gently in Mrs. O'Leary's mind.

"I'll remember that," she replied, getting her emotions under control. Nellie was safe; that was what was important. "This is my house, however, Mr. Ovani. I do not need your permission to take in any guest."

Of course not, but it would help keep yourself

and the young girl safe.

Hard to argue with that logic. "These beings who cast illusions aren't supposed to be on Earth, are they?"

No. They are forbidden to come here. This one thought he could take advantage of my distraction. There was something like a smile in Mrs. O'Leary's mind. *He didn't believe a human would be able to see through his illusions. He knew that soon I was not going to be as distracted. I suspect he planned one more feeding before he left.*

"Pain fed him?"

For the most part, yes. His kind also eats dead carcasses. A scavenger.

Mrs. O'Leary didn't want to think about what she ate. "Thank you, Mr. Ovani."

There definitely was a smile in her mind. *For what? You had already taken care of the matter before I arrived.*

"Thank you for being here," Mrs. O'Leary said in all honesty. "I don't doubt a lot more of the bad types would show up here if'n it weren't for you."

Perhaps.

The colors shifted and Katie thought she could see a distant star and then Mr. Ovani was gone. Up to his room, or wherever he really lived.

Lost and Found

Katie sat at her small desk off the back parlor, reviewing her accounts. Sunlight sparkled through the round stained glass window; it was just after noon.

Allowing herself a small smile, Katie leaned back in the large oak chair. It had been a good year for her boarding house. All her boarders were up to date on their room-and-board accounts. There was more gold in the basement she'd melt down soon, but that was a good problem to have.

It was worth dealing with strange people to have such financial security. Even if she'd a giant cockroach and what looked like an enormous slug as boarders.

As she worked on the accounts, Katie listened for any sign that her niece, Nellie, had found something she shouldn't. Nellie was a good, hard worker and it would have been difficult to take care of the large house on her own, but Nellie could never learn exactly who—or what—the boarders were. Give the girl a fit of the vapors, it would. Not that Nellie was the type to have vapors. She was a strapping no-nonsense girl of nearly fifteen now.

With that thought, Nellie came through the back parlor, shaking her head. That was never a good sign.

"What's the matter, girl?" Katie asked.

"A cat. On the front porch. A real cat, not that six-legged thing in bedroom six, which I am sure is not a birth defect."

Nellie might be getting a bit too smart.

"What sort of cat?" Katie asked. "What's he doing?"

"What do ya mean—what sort of cat? A big cat, that's for sure. And he is just sitting there. Bold as brass," Nellie continued as she went through the back parlor and into the kitchen, coming out with a broom.

"What color cat?" Katie asked.

"What does it matter? I'll get rid of 'im."

"It might matter very much," Katie said firmly. It would be most odd if a Cat was here, but stranger things had happened. In this very house.

"He's grey." Nellie went down the hallway towards the front door.

Katie was up quickly. She caught up to her niece and grabbed the broom. "I'll take care of this, girl. You've done your work for the day. Maybe best you went home."

"I ain't got the dusting half-done," the girl protested.

"Haven't got," Mrs. O'Leary corrected her.

Girl picked up too much of her language from her pa who had almost no education. "Well, I'm fine with what you've gotten done today," Katie was firm. "You head on home now. Out the back way."

"Pa's house is out the front way."

"Don't you back talk me girl! The back door is good enough. The Cat may misunderstand if'n you go out the front."

"What does a cat matter?"

Katie just took the broom and turned the girl around. A grey Cat indeed. Mr. Marlet, the six-legged cat, who was not really a cat, talked about Cats sometimes. Talked about how very important they were. Katie was not quite sure why or even where they were important. Maybe they were important everywhere but on Earth. Mr. Marlet made it clear that having a Cat as a guest was something most people hoped for. Whole generations might hope for that even.

Very respectable, Cats were, he said.

It would be good to have more respectable boarders.

Katie opened the heavy, thick oak door with the leaded glass window. Sure enough, a Cat sat on her front porch. She knew what they looked like because Mr. Marlet had bowed to an alley cat once in mistake.

It was big for a regular cat for sure. Sat there all regal like. Mrs. O'Leary wasn't one for bowing, but she did graciously nod her head. The

Cat's paw came up. Dangling from a claw (was the claw gold?) was the red universal translator disc. Katie knew the routine and gave her name and address so the translator could get a fix on the language.

The disk hummed for a moment and then blinked a couple of times. Katie knew that meant it understood the language.

"You have rooms?" the Cat purred.

Katie did have a room available, on the second floor where all the boarders lived, but it was small. The Cat didn't look like the type who stayed in small rooms.

Katie thought a moment. If she could advertise that she had a Cat stay with her, what would that be worth? Likely she could raise her rates. Well, for that Katie could give up her own large bedroom on the first floor.

"Yes, I do. Would you like to come in?" She stepped back and held the door open.

The Cat slipped the universal translator into a pouch by his neck. He walked into the entryway and stopped to look around. The Cat was very graceful in his movements. All cats were, but this one even more so.

The Cat sniffed the air a little and looked into the front parlor. The sliding door was open. The large room beyond was well-crafted with carved oak paneling and a cheap but serviceable Persian carpet. The large front window had the drapes pulled close.

"Very....quaint." The Cat made a sound between a meow and a purr.

"Yes, most of my guests are pleased with the arrangement."

The Cat looked a bit puzzled. "Yes, of course."

"Would you like to see the room? Actually I have two rooms available. One is large and downstairs and the other one is smaller and upstairs."

"Does the downstairs room have a window?"

Mrs. O'Leary hadn't thought of that. Cats did like windows. "No. The downstairs room doesn't have any windows, but it is larger."

"I will see them both."

"How should I address you?" It was the standard question she used.

"I am a Cat."

"Yes, Mr. Marlet has explained about Cats. I was inquiring about your name."

The Cat stopped his inspection of the entryway and oak staircase. He stared up at her. "We do not know each other well enough for you to address me as anything other than Cat." Tone was sometimes tricky with the universal translator, but there didn't seem to be any doubt that Mr. Cat did not feel they would _ever_ know each other well enough to go beyond Mr. Cat.

Well, she could accept that.

Katie led the way to her bedroom off the back parlor, alongside the dining room. The room was spacious and had another Persian rug.

The Cat barely looked at it. "Too dark. I'll take the other room."

"But you haven't seen it."

The Cat tilted his head towards her. "I have seen this one. It is unacceptable. The other one must be acceptable. You said it had a window."

"Yes, but..."

"I require a window."

"As you wish. It is upstairs." Katie and the Cat walked back down the hallway to the oak staircase. "The cost of the room...is two dollars a week." Actually she let that room for a dollar and a quarter, but she thought the Cat might appreciate it more if it was more expensive. "Will you be requiring board?"

The Cat paused halfway up the staircase. "Why would I require wood?"

Universal translator problems again.

"Will you require me to cook your meals?"

The Cat visibly shuddered. "My meals will be delivered nightly."

"Has to be late night. The neighbors have too much to talk about already."

"I understand this is a very backward place."

"The United States is as good as any country," Katie hotly defended her adopted country. Ireland was a good country too, but the United States was second to none.

The Cat stopped again, puzzled. "I know of no

united states. And what is a 'country'?"

Mrs. O'Leary sighed. "Nevermind. There is an ice box in the barn behind the house. Mr. Longger can show your people where it is. I just had ice delivered today, so whatever is delivered will stay cool overnight." She paused for a moment. "It won't be alive, will it? The meals, I mean. If they are, we need to make another arrangement."

The Cat stopped at the top of the stairs to stare at her again.

"Mr. Szmch has live meals delivered twice a week," Katie explained. "I cook them just as he asks. But live meals are a bit of a problem."

"I had heard the deposed *ittilig* Emperor was in exile here. I believe I also heard that an Ovani resides here."

"Mr. Ovani does have a room. I cook his meals as well."

The Cat smiled. "Interesting. I should like to talk to...him."

It took the translator a bit longer than usual to decide on the gender designation. Not surprising.

"That will be up to him. The guests usually meet together in the front parlor on Sunday afternoons. This is Tuesday. The meeting will be in four more days, umm, solar cycles."

The Cat made no reply. Maybe didn't understand. Not that it mattered that much. Mrs. O'Leary would explain again as the day got closer.

They were at the small room the cockroach had taken for five months. After he had moved to the attic, and then died – well, been killed by a bounty hunter – Katie had thoroughly cleaned it. Twice.

She opened the door and stepped back to let the Cat enter.

The Cat walked in and turned around. Without saying anything Mrs. O'Leary had the feeling the Cat thought the room smaller than any closet back home.

The Cat reached into the fur pouch at his neck and took out a large gold coin. Katie noticed his claws definitely were tinted with gold. He held the coin out to her. It would pay for more than a year! Maybe even two years.

"I have nothing smaller," the Cat stated with some arrogance. As though it would be beneath him to carry smaller gold coins.

Certainly an arrogant Cat, but for that much gold he could be as arrogant as he liked. Katie took the coin. It was a bit unusual. Even for a gold coin from outer space. One side had the profile of a cat and the other some alien writing. Mrs. O'Leary had never had a cat coin before. Lovely coin, it was. Maybe she'd wait a bit before melting it down.

"I wish to speak with the Ovani," the cat purred.

"Mr. Ovani normally keeps to himself."

"Which room is he in?"

The Cat was going to be a difficult boarder, Mrs. O'Leary could already tell that. "I'll ask him if he wants company," she said firmly. "All my guests have a right to privacy."

Mr. Ovani's room was just two down and across the hall. Mrs. O'Leary tapped on his door. "Mr. Ovani? A Cat wishes to speak with you?"

A claw opened the door, then it became misty and a series of tentacles and then two fingers.

That will be all, Mrs. O'Leary. He thought at her.

The Cat was right beside her. Mrs. O'Leary almost tripped as she turned around. The Cat hopped to one side, hissing. Katie almost told the Cat to leave. Her boarders did not hiss at her.

Mr. Ovani thought at her again, apologizing for the Cat. Temperamental they were, and this one more than most.

So Mr. Ovani knew this Cat. That made a bit of a difference. Katie couldn't think he would know disreputable people.

The Cat stared at Mr. Ovani who thought back at it. Because she was still so close, Katie caught part of their conversation. Something was lost and if it wasn't found, then spaceships would...well, she couldn't tell exactly what the spaceships were doing, there were so many colors, but she gathered it wouldn't be good and she didn't think spaceships should explode in any case.

Katie went back down the staircase. They really hadn't settled exactly when, and what, the Cat's grocer would deliver. Katie preferred to have some idea what these meals might be. She wasn't unreasonable, but Mr. Szmch's slugs were about the limit of what she'd deal with. If the Cat thought she could have live rats delivered, or worse, dead ones, then they'd have to have a talk.

Mrs. O'Leary looked again at the lovely gold coin. She just might not melt this one down at all. Jewelry-like it was.

Chapter 2

Katie didn't see any more of the Cat for the rest of the morning and into the afternoon. It was getting near supper time; she was fighting with Mr. Smzch's slugs again. She was a little out of sorts. It was the Cat. So arrogant he was. She hit the middle-sized slug a good whap! It fell back into the pan clearly dead. She'd hit it a bit too hard. Well, she was tired of fighting with the slugs; tired of trying to cook them just right. Mr. Smzch paid well and was nice, but still a man should eat proper food, not slugs!

But Mr. Smzch was not a man.

The slugs settled down. They needed just another moment or two. Mr. Smzch was very particular the slugs be only slightly cooked.

"Mrs. O'Leary?" The Cat stood in the doorway of the kitchen.

"Just a moment. I have to finish up Mr. Smzch's dinner."

Surprisingly, the Cat just sat down and waited.

Katie spooned the slugs into the wide dish and put them to one side. She'd need to bring them upstairs soon. Mr. Smzch didn't like cold slugs.

"What do you need?" Katie suddenly realized she hadn't shown the Cat the bathroom. Did a Cat use one? Or did he need something else?

The Cat tilted his head to one side, as though puzzled.

Could it read her thoughts? It was bad enough Mr. Ovani could, but a Cat?

"I need to go outside."

Well, that was where most cats did their business.

"I'd prefer you not use the flower bed." Mrs. O'Leary picked up the dish of slugs and added the black powder sprinkles Mr. Szmch liked.

The Cat looked puzzled again. "I need to go around this...area. I am looking for...something."

Were cats really that fussy about where they did their...business? "Well, you do look like a large cat, so maybe you can walk around a bit outside in daylight. It would be better at night but if you have to go now, then don't leave the property. People might not understand. I mean they may mistake you for a regular cat."

The Cat's fur rose a little. "I am no 'regular' cat." The sound he made was closer to a growl.

"No, of course not. Certainly not any cat we are used to here."

The fur lay back down. "I understand this planet has animals like us in feature, but smaller."

"Yes, we have rather a few cats. I used to keep a cat here to help keep down the mice."

The Cat looked puzzled. "How does one keep a cat?"

Mrs. O'Leary smiled. "Mostly you just have to feed them. And cats here like to be petted; they like a nice lap."

The Cat continued to look puzzled, then shook his head. "I have to look around outside. How do I get back inside when I'm done?"

It wasn't a problem she usually had. Most times, her guests stayed inside. Likely end up in a freak show if'n people saw them. The Cat, however large, was visually just a rather large domestic cat.

"There is a smaller door in the middle of large door out to the back steps." Mrs. O'Leary pointed to the door at one side of the kitchen that led out to the back stairs. "I usually leave that small door unlatched in the day, but if you'll be out late, I'll leave it unlatched. You can come right in through that. I'd appreciate if you'd latch it after you come in."

"I will do that," the Cat meowed, slipping through the small door. Katie watched the cat trot down the wide back steps. He started making a mewing sound. Not unlike a mom cat calling her kittens.

Odd Cat he was, no doubt about it. She picked up the plate of slugs and took them up the back stairs to Mr. Smzch.

Katie waited for the Cat to return. She really preferred her guests to stay inside. Who knew what could happen to a Cat in Chicago? Evening turned into night and still the Cat did not return. Katie went back upstairs to Mr. Ovani's room and tapped on the door. She hated to disturb him, but she really was worried. While it would be good to be able to advertise that a Cat had chosen her rooming house, it would obviously be very bad if the Cat was killed.

Mr. Ovani opened the door. He was feathered at first and then shifted to fingers. Katie had the feeling she was interrupting something. Nothing definite; it was just he seemed a bit distracted. It took longer than usual to change to fingers and a little more human appearance.

Most unusual to see you twice in one day, Mr. Ovani thought at her.

Katie couldn't tell if that was a rebuke or not. "Well, sorry I am to intrude again, but the Cat has gone out and hasn't come back. He said he wanted to go outside, but that was over three

hours ago. Can't take that long to do his
business." Katie always spoke. She just preferred
that to thinking at someone. Thinking at a
person just didn't seem right.

*Her business might take much longer than a
few hours, Mrs. O'Leary. I suggest you go to bed.
Cats can take care of themselves very well.
Especially that one.*

Her? Oh, well, Katie wasn't going to think
about that just now. She had a feeling they were
talking about two different kinds of business, but
that didn't matter. "Can you tell if he is all
right?"

Mr. Ovani tilted his...well, now it was sort of
head-like. *For now she is all right. But she must
do what she came here to do. It is very important.*

"Sorry to disturb you again," Mrs. O'Leary
said politely.

Mr. Ovani gently closed the door. With a
tentacle.

Katie went back down the steps. She waited
in the kitchen as the hours slipped by.

It was getting near midnight. Far past her
usual bed time.

The small door set in the bottom of the larger
door swung open and the Cat entered the
kitchen. She stopped, surprised to see her. "I
thought your people slept at night?" the Cat
meowed at her.

Mrs. O'Leary stood up, more than a little
tired. "I don't like to sleep while my guests are

still outside. It isn't always a hospitable place, here in Chicago, for different kinds of...people."

The Cat made a purring sound. "Quite kind of you, but I will be going outside regularly. I have to find something...that was lost. Something very valuable."

"Well, I'm not sure why you think whatever you are looking for is around here, but Mr. Ovani said much the same thing. Still, I wouldn't want anything to happen to you." Mrs. O'Leary stepped out onto the back porch and turned the wick all the way down on the lantern she'd left hanging over the back door. Entering the kitchen again, she closed the door behind her, setting the latch on the full door and the small door. "Good night," she told the Cat.

The Cat tilted her head as though she would say something more. After a moment, she meowed softly. "If there is a problem, Mrs. O'Leary, it might be difficult for you to handle."

"I'm not some frail, smelling salts type of lady." Indeed, Katie was not quite forty, still chopped most of her own wood, (from larger pieces to smaller ones, true; she'd never cut down a whole tree) and had relied on herself most of her life.

The Cat stared at her for a long moment, purred a bit and then gracefully walked towards the stairs. "Good night Mrs. O'Leary."

Chapter 3

Katie took out the lovely gold coin the Cat had given her. She wanted to look at it again; she needed to remember how lovely it was. She had been staying up far too late every night waiting for her boarder to come back from wherever it was that she went, looking for whatever it was that was lost.

It had been over a week, and still the Cat went out every night, coming back later and later. Katie wasn't sure how long she could manage this. Also it seemed the Cat was getting into fights. She came in bleeding twice, and even when she wasn't bleeding her fur was almost always matted like she had been looking in dark and dirty places. Always doing that low meow call that the universal translator did not translate.

The Cat had not come to the Sunday gathering. Mrs. O'Leary had proudly told all her guests about the Cat, but it had not produced the results she had hoped. Her other boarders had exchanged looks that she could only think were worried. Hard to be sure of expression when it's an octopus, but the six-legged cat had put down his hookah for a long moment, nodding almost sadly. "The Gurset is lost."

Well, they obviously understood something

she didn't. She had no idea what a Gurset was. And she had learned that sometimes it was better not to ask. She had simply let the conversation move on. At least she learned the Cat was looking for something called Gurset. That was two days ago.

It was getting near 2 a.m. Katie got up to put a kettle on for more water for tea. The wood in the stove had cooled to hot embers. Ideal for steeping tea.

"YEOWLL!"

The cry came from her backyard. A cat fight of enormous proportions. And her guest was out there.

Mrs. O'Leary didn't hesitate. She ran to the back door, picking up the baseball bat she kept by for just such needs. She'd had to use it once to defend one of her human boarders years ago; she could do it again.

She flung open the back door. In front of the bottom step was her Cat, rearing up on her back legs, (it was definitely a she) her claws fully extended, her fur standing up.

"YEOWLL!" Cat screamed again.

The Cat was facing another very large Cat, a dirty mottled black Cat, and two grey dogs that were more the size of wolves. At her feet, the Cat was sheltering a bedraggled kitten. A calico kitten. The highest rank of Cats, Mr. Marlet had told her. It was larger than most cats found in Chicago, but clearly a kitten.

Mrs. O'Leary went down the three steps to stand beside the Cat, her baseball bat at her shoulders. "I don't know who, or what, you are," she told the attackers, "but this is my house and my guest, and you had best leave while you can."

The mottled black Cat snarled an answer that the communicator didn't translate. It wasn't necessary. The black wolves grinned showing enormous teeth.

"This is beyond your abilities," the Cat said softly. "Retreat."

"Damned if I will," Katie stated, not caring that she swore. "Three to one, you can't win." She stepped a bit closer to the kitten. If that was what they were after, they'd have to go through her.

The wolf on the right, closest to her, growled deep in his throat. "You will be a tasty tidbit." He leapt at her as the black Cat launched at her guest and the other wolf dove for the kitten.

Mrs. O'Leary swung at the wolf's ribcage, stepping forward to add more power to the swing. She'd learned that in Ireland. She knocked him back hard. He rolled on the grass, snarling, then quickly snapped back to his feet. On her left, the Cat seemed to be taking on both the black Cat and the other wolf, slashing with all her claws out, rolling and snarling in the grass.

Katie had little time for the grey Cat as the wolf lunged, mouth open, growling deep in his chest, aiming for her throat. She tilted the bat back, taking a deep frightened breath.

Suddenly there was a blackness beyond anything she could imagine; stars, burned like pinpoints in the distance, but desolation surrounded her. It was a place where no sun had ever shone.

She almost screamed in terror; she was falling down into that place. Then she was in her backyard. Gas jets were being turned up in the neighbors' houses. Voices yelling, but for a moment she couldn't take anything in. She could still see and feel the complete emptiness of space.

Then Mr. Ovani was standing next to her, his black cape thrown wide. In the cape was the darkness where there was no sun. His body had no shape; there was only the cloak with the space between the stars.

Her corset was much too tight; she couldn't breathe.

Mr. Camber, her neighbor to the south, crossed over the small lawns. "Mrs. O'Leary, are you all right?"

Her neighbors quite settled her fears. She had to protect her guests. He must not see Mr. Ovani!

She looked towards him, to warn him, but standing at her side was an older gentleman with fine grey hair. Very distinguished looking, he was. Holding silver headed, ebony cane.

"Mrs. O'Leary! Are you all right?" Mr. Camber repeated. Several of her neighbors left their houses and began to crowd into her small backyard.

Katie took as deep a breath as her corset would allow, steadying her jumbled thoughts. There were no wolves, no large black cat. Just her and Mr. Ovani, and the Cat and kitten.

The Cat picked up the kitten, much like any Chicago cat would, by the nap of its neck, and slipped inside. Only her and Mr. Ovani stood on her back step.

"Very unusual sound," Mr. Ovani said calmly. "Never heard anything like it. Did it come from the alley back there?"

"I thought it came from right here!" Mr. Camber stated.

"No, I'm sure it was in the alley," Mr. Ovani countered mildly. "We saw nothing here that would cause such a racket."

The neighbors looked around. It was true; there was nothing but the half dozen of them in the backyard.

"Sounded like the gates of hell opening up," Mrs. Abernathy stated, her dressing gown pulled close around her. Her husband stepped closer to her. "It did indeed," he agreed.

"So very odd," Mr. Ovani commented. "I cannot think the gates of hell would open up here."

That made the neighbors look a bit

embarrassed. Chicago might not be a place of heavenly virtue, but surely not a place where hell lived so near?

"I don't believe we've met," the widow Smith said, stepping up to the back porch, looking intently at Mr. Ovani.

Oh, of course she would go right for him, Katie thought unkindly. Remembering her manners, though, she did the appropriate introductions. "Mrs. Smith, this is one of my boarders, Mr. Ovani. Mr. Ovani, my neighbor, Mrs. Smith."

"The widow Mrs. Smith," the woman added quickly while smiling. "I am quite sure we've never met. I would remember such a handsome man. You should come by for some of my apple pie. Best in the whole city, if I do say so myself."

"I thank you," Mr. Ovani said gallantly, with a slight bow. "Perhaps I shall. Mrs. O'Leary, though, does set such a fine repast, I rarely need any more sustenance."

The widow blinked. Katie wasn't sure what surprised the widow more: the gallantry, or the words Mr. Ovani used. *Sustenance* wasn't a word heard often in her neighborhood.

"Well, whatever that noise was, it is gone now," Mr. Ovani pointed out. He held out his arm to Mrs. O'Leary. "I'm sure we will all be better for seeking our beds."

Katie put her hand on Mr. Ovani's arm, not sure if it would change to a tentacle or who knows what, but it remained an arm as they walked inside.

The Cat was in the kitchen grooming the kitten, licking him thoroughly. The kitten didn't seem to mind at all. The only sounds were purring.

The Cat looked up at Mrs. O'Leary. "You stood to fight at my side," she meowed. "And against two *humri*, that takes courage."

Mrs. O'Leary was about to tell her she wasn't the type to let anyone—anything—attack her guests.

"My name is Merapet," the Cat stated. "I am the Guardian of the Gurset." She indicated with a lick that the kitten was the Gurset. "He is the heir to the Hisrow throne."

"Very nice to meet you," Mrs. O'Leary said formally. "My name is Katie. I take it you came here looking for him."

"Yes. He is the heir to a large empire. He was kidnapped by a traitor in the palace and given to the *humri*. If I did not bring him back, there would have been war with the *humri*." The Cat paused in its grooming. "I am trained in many forms of combat. I have never seen a weapon like you had. What is it called?"

Katie gave a shaky laugh. "A baseball bat. Technically it isn't a weapon, but it can be useful in a fight." Her thoughts were still a jumble, and she was shaking just a bit. Not from fear. It was just that so much had happened so swiftly. Or at least that's what she told herself, although she had to admit it would be a long time before she would forget that *humri's* mouth, opened wide, drooling and snarling.

"Why would you think the Gurset was here?" Katie focused on the simplest part of the whole situation.

"The Ovani told us a *humri* ship came here recently. They thought the ship would not be noticed."

Katie looked at Mr. Ovani. He was still the handsome silver-haired man he had been outside.

"You prefer this form?" he asked, using words.

Katie nodded. "Yes, if you do not mind."

Mr. Ovani smiled. "I shall take this form then whenever you are around."

The kitten mewed softly; it was like a cry.

"Oh, dear. He is hungry. They have not been feeding him much at all," Merapet meowed.

"I have some fresh milk I purchased yesterday from one of my neighbors," Katie offered. She had been going to make butter, but that could wait.

Merapet looked at the Ovani who nodded. "It will suffice."

Katie opened the door to the ice box and got out the heavy pitcher. The cream had risen to the top. "Would the cream be good for him?" she asked Mr. Ovani.

"Quite good. Heating it a little would be best," he added.

Mrs. O'Leary stirred the cream in and then poured a small bowl full. She started towards her stove, where the wood still glowed.

"That isn't necessary, Mrs. O'Leary." Mr. Ovani took the bowl in his hands and within seconds the chill was gone. He put it down by the Gurset who was now standing, somewhat wobbly, on all four paws.

Clearly he had no idea of what had just been put in front of him. He looked at his Guardian who nodded. The kitten gave a tentative lick, then quickly lapped the bowl dry.

"Meow!" he said. He wasn't quite close enough to the translator, but Katie could still understand.

"He is very pleased with this dish. He would like some more if that is possible?"

"Yes, of course." Katie poured more into the bowl and Mr. Ovani heated it. The kitten lapped that up as well.

"That should be enough for him." Mr. Ovani said.

The kitten curled up in a ball, contentedly purring.

"Will you be leaving soon?" Mrs. O'Leary asked. She had thought the Cat was a difficult guest, but now she understood more.

"Yes, a ship will be coming tonight to take us

home." Merapet paused as though uncertain of her next words. "When he is grown, may I bring him back to you? I think he would like to thank you himself for all you've done."

Katie smiled. "I didn't do anything but give him some cream."

"No, you stood at my side. I saw you move forward to protect him. Your intention was quite clear. You are a credit to your species, Katie."

Katie wasn't quite clear what a 'species' was, but she understood what Merapet meant. "Yes, I'd like to see him when he is grown."

"And we might have to occasionally buy some of this liquid that he obviously likes so much."

Katie nodded. "I would like that as well." Not only was her house now Cat approved, but she could say with all honesty that she provided food for the Gurset, heir to the throne of Hisrow.

Beauty

The sun hadn't been up for an hour, but the temperature was rising quickly. It was going to a warm one for sure. A bit early in June for such heat.

Katie opened the front door to let a little breeze in. She'd close it before it got too hot.

She was surprised to see Mr. Ovani sitting on the front porch swing. In his human form, of course.

She almost commented on his being up early, but since she doubted he ever slept, that would have been a ridiculous thing to say.

"Good morning, Mr. Ovani," she settled for.

"Ah, Mrs. O'Leary, I was hoping you would be up soon." Sometimes when Mr. Ovani took human form, he spoke rather than thought at her. Mrs. O'Leary definitely preferred that.

In fact she had been up over an hour, getting breakfast ready and straightening up a bit. No need to bother him with such details, though.

Katie noticed that he had an ornate box in his lap, with wide screens on the side. She stared at it for a moment, a bit worried.

"I've brought you a new guest," he said.

The box wasn't very big. That was what worried her. Whatever could he have in there? "A new guest, Mr. Ovani?"

"Indeed, Mrs. O'Leary, one I think you will like very much."

"He's a bit small." She voiced her concern. Katie hoped Mr. Ovani hadn't brought her another bug. She wasn't a bigot, but she just couldn't warm up to bugs.

You might change your mind with this one. The words floated through her mind.

"Any guest you recommend, I'm sure I will like."

Well, let us go inside. Yarwoos like sunshine, but here the sun might be too bright. I didn't want to risk her coming to harm.

Her? That could be a problem. She never took in female boarders. Well, Merapet was female, but Katie hadn't known that at first. Besides, Merapet was a cat. Like a leopard was a cat.

Still, how was she going to explain to the other gentlemen?

What was she thinking of? None of her boarders were human. The old rules didn't apply any more.

I should think not, Mr. Ovani offered.

Chicago society in the late 1860s considered it immoral for a woman to live in a rooming house with men. Oddly, it was not considered at all improper for a widowed woman to run a boarding house for gentlemen. Mrs. O'Leary, before taking in aliens, had always lived by this social code.

With the minor exception that she wasn't really a widow. No one ever asked about a Mr. O'Leary, and in fact there never had been one. When Katie immigrated to the United States, using money from selling the family bar, she decided it would be easier for her in the new country if she was a widow, and so she changed her name, adding a Mrs in front. Simple really, and it gave her considerably more freedom.

Her sister, Mary, who followed her a year later knew the truth of course, but she never told anyone. Mary had found love in the new world. And death in childbirth.

Nellie, Mary's firstborn child, was as dear to her as her sister had been. Someday Katie might tell Nellie the truth about her guests, but for now, the less the girl knew the better.

Katie gave herself a mental shake. Her mind had been awandering. The gender of the new guest wasn't important. 'Specially if she was a bug.

"Well, let's go in then." She always spoke to Mr. Ovani. She held the door open for him. He smiled. Katie smiled back. Here was a being who likely could shatter worlds and she was holding the door for him like he was an invalid.

"The back parlor, I think," Mr. Ovani said. "You've got that large south facing window."

"I have a room upstairs that is available. The

window isn't as large..."

"You will want her downstairs."

Katie felt tempted to remind him she did like some privacy, but instead followed him into the back parlor, the one reserved for family gatherings.

He opened the ornate carved wood door and a butterfly flitted out. To say it was a butterfly was to say the Mississippi was a stream. It wasn't the size; she wasn't much larger than a large butterfly, similar to a hummingbird. It was, well, she was so much more than a large butterfly.

The *Yarwoo* paused on the edge of the ornate box, her wings unfolding. Translucent, they were. Large, too, for her small body. Then the sunlight hit the wings.

Katie inhaled, and then stopped breathing entirely. Rainbows filled the room, shimmering off the *Yarwoos* wings. Rainbows with colors she didn't even know existed, colors that had no name.

It took a moment before Katie remembered to breathe again. She sat down. On the floor. Staring at the beauty that filled the small parlor.

"Oh, my," she managed to get out.

There is no being who does not love a Yarwoo. Even those who cannot see color.

Katie might have questioned that except the *Yarwoo* started to fly, slow, graceful swoops and dives. "Ooh."

Time slipped by unnoticed. Sunset came and the *Yarwoo* flitted to the windowsill to catch the last of the sun's rays. The *Yarwoo* had a slender grey body with six legs, and a small head. Katie didn't see any eyes, but maybe they weren't necessary. Or were too small to be easily seen. Didn't matter.

Mr. Ovani made a soft trilling sound and the Yarwoo came to his hand.

Katie woke as if from a dream. "What time?" Before she could lift her watch pendant, the hall clock struck 8 p.m.

"Oh, my. Mr. Szmch's dinner." She might have asked where the day had gone, but she knew, and had no regrets, except Mr. Szmch would be testy. He liked his supper at six p.m. That brought up another thought.

"What does she eat?" If it had been liquid gold, Katie would not have minded.

Sunlight, Mr. Ovani replied.

"Do you think she would like the front bedroom upstairs?"

"She will be fine here. A nice box with something soft will suit her very well." Mr. Ovani looked around the room. *On the top shelf of that bookcase.*

"I'll get that..." she was going to say right after Mr. Szmch's dinner, but he could wait. After all it was already late.

Katie went into her bedroom. She had something in mind. On top of her bureau was a small carved walnut jewelry box. She transferred the jewelry to her underwear drawer and found a nice, soft, flannel washcloth. She used it to pad the box and brought it back to the back parlor.

"Will this work?"

Mr. Ovani held out his hand. The *Yarwoo* tilted her head, stared for a long moment and then glided gracefully over to it.

Mrs. O'Leary was unreasonably thrilled. She carefully carried the box to the top shelf of the bookcase.

The *Yarwoo* made a soft trilling sound and curled up to sleep.

"She is so wonderful! Thank you for bringing her here."

"It was for her sake I suggested she come here."

"Is she in some problem?"

"Her species is. There are very few Yarwoo left. They need a particular type of sunlight and there are not many worlds with the exact right sun. Her world was destroyed millennia ago. I hoped Earth would be one of those where she might thrive, and obviously I was correct."

"Will she stay long?"

"Just the summer. The winters here are too cold and there is too little sun. She would die."

"Then she must go after summer!"

Mr. Ovani turned to Mrs. O'Leary. He looked so like a handsome, slightly elderly gentleman,

Katie had to smile. "You are a credit to your species, Mrs. O'Leary."

If he were human she might have thought he was flattering her.

Mr. Ovani smiled back. "Mr. Szmch's supper is late. If you will get the...I believe you call them slugs, I will take care of cooking it."

"That is my job, Mr. Ovani. It won't take me long to get the wood and get the stove going."

"And after that, you must boil the sauce with the...slugs." Mr. Ovani shook his head. "I have made you late tonight. This is a very small thing for me to do."

Katie wasn't quite sure what he meant to do, but she went to the barn and and got a box of slugs. It was quite difficult to say 'no' to Mr. Ovani.

"Put them in the bowl."

Mrs. O'Leary tipped them in. They immediately started scrambling to get out. Mr. Ovani hummed a moment and they were still. He held the bowl between his hands. "Pour the sauce in."

She did. In a moment, the bowl was steaming. "That's remarkable."

Mr. Ovani gave a very human-like chuckle. "A small thing, Mrs. O'Leary." He handed the bowl back to her and she sprinkled the black powder on it.

"Thank you, Mr. Ovani. You saved me

time...and work."

Mr. Ovani bowed slightly and turned to go up the front steps. Katie went up the back steps to Mr. Szmch's room and tapped on the door. She let herself in, carefully holding the bowl of slugs.

"Late with my supper, Mrs. O'Leary," Mr. Szmch stated disagreeably. "I do not appreciate my meal arriving late."

"I am sorry, but..." Katie tried to think of how to explain that she lost track of time, that watching rainbows scattered across the back parlor...well, there was no explaining and no excusing.

"I know the Ovani brought a *Yarwoo*. People seem to lose their minds around them." He made a small hole in the force field and snatched his dinner in. "They're nothing but a parasitic insect."

"Oh, I quite disagree."

"Don't make a habit of being late with my supper," Mr. Szmch stated as the force field closed.

Katie stood in the small outer room and took a deep breath to calm her temper. She had been tempted to ask him: Or what?

That would have been rude. She would try to do better, but she would make no promises. Not with a *Yarwoo* in the house.

Chapter 2

The sun wasn't quite up, but Mrs. O'Leary was already at work. In the two days since the *Yarwoo* arrived, she had learned if she was going to get any of her work done around the house, it had to be before the sun came up. Afterwards, well, it just didn't happen.

Katie was quite content to sit in the back parlor and watch the beautiful colors dance across her walls. She was folding wash she had done the previous evening when she heard the sweet trilling that meant the *Yarwoo* was rising. She put the pillowcases down and went to the parlor.

The *Yarwoo* was uncurling from her bed. Gracefully, as she did everything. The sunlight was beginning to stream through the south facing window as Katie settled in her favorite chair.

The Yarwoo trilled again as she took flight. Katie didn't even hear the back door open and close a few minutes later.

"Auntie?" Nellie called.

Mrs. O'Leary turned her head, for a moment not realizing who called her, so deeply in thrall was she.

"Ooh!" Nellie stood in the doorway to the back parlor.

Katie belatedly remembered the day was

Saturday. That's when Nellie came in the morning to help with the cleaning.

Nellie slowly walked into the room and settled on the floor by her aunt's feet. Katie laid a gentle hand on the girl's shoulder.

In a moment or two, it seemed, nightfall came. The *Yarwoo* flew to Mr. Ovani, touched him with a light wing and then to Mrs. O'Leary. She touched her as well with the tip of a wing on her cheek. Then flew to her box and curled up for the night.

"Oh, my." Nellie spoke first.

Katie nodded. She certainly understood. "Nellie, you cannot tell anyone about this. Ever."

The girl rose to her feet and held her hands out to help her aunt up. Sitting for so long made Katie's joints a bit stiff. "Auntie, I never tell anyone anything I see here. Who would believe it?"

Girl had a point.

Nellie looked around the parlor. "Auntie, we have a bit of work to do here."

Katie saw the dust, which she never liked, being particular about the cleanliness of her house, but this time she just shrugged. "I'll get up earlier tomorrow and do the dusting."

"If I come by early as well and help, can I stay?"

Katie nodded. "Tell your father I need you a bit more this summer."

"Thank you, auntie!"

Katie wasn't one for emotional displays, finding them rather vulgar, but she gave Nellie a quick hug and a kiss on the top of her head. The girl blushed with pleasure.

"Before you go, Nellie, would you get a box of slugs from the barn. And if the cow says anything, just ignore him."

"I always do."

"I'll heat the meal tonight again," Mr. Ovani offered.

"I hate to put you to the effort."

"It is no effort, Mrs. O'Leary. Heat is simply a form of energy."

Katie wasn't sure what he meant by that, but it didn't matter. It would help. Mr. Szmch was getting more testy each evening. She'd have a piece of cold chicken and some pickled vegetables she'd put up the previous summer. No need to start a fire in the stove at all.

June slipped by and half of July. Nellie was over most days. Her father wasn't too pleased, but the extra money Katie sent home with Nellie helped. Mr. Szmch got used to late meals and Mr. Ovani most often heated them up.

Katie told Mr. Ovani, with a slight blush, that he was spoiling her and she would start to get lazy. Mr. Ovani said that was unlikely.

Katie wasn't so sure. Never had so much housekeeping slipped by, undone, unnoticed really. Her guests didn't complain and likely didn't even care since the Sunday afternoons they were downstairs for the weekly gatherings, they spent the time watching the *Yarwoo* as well. Even Mr. Szmch liked the patterns playing across the walls although he admitted he couldn't see any colors.

Things changed half-way through July. The *Yarwoo* began to sing.

How could such a small creature, not much larger than a hummingbird, sing so loudly? It wasn't really singing; it was more soft, sweet notes, floating up and down. No words, just music. Complex music.

The first time Katie heard it she stopped breathing. She forced herself to turn to Mr. Ovani. "What?" was all she could manage.

"The best news possible. The *Yarwoo* is pregnant. That is why she sings."

Katie glanced at Nellie. People didn't openly discuss pregnancy. Even the word itself was...well, not particularly polite.

Nellie's eyes were wide, but with wonder.

Katie turned back to Mr. Ovani. After all, the girl had been raised around animals; she had to understand the concept at least a little. "How is that possible? Is there another *Yarwoo* here?"

Mr. Ovani's smile was gentle. He didn't look away from the *Yarwoo*. "*Yarwoos* become pregnant when there is enough sunlight."

"Oh." Katie remembered there were very few

Yarwoo left. "This is very good, right? It isn't a problem that she is here on Earth?"

"The sunlight here is what made her pregnant. If the sun light is strong enough for a long enough time, she will give birth."

"But here? Is that safe?" However proud she might be of the United States, Katie understand it was very primitive by her boarders' standards.

"I will be here. I will keep her safe."

That was good enough for her. Mrs. O'Leary settled back in her chair and enjoyed the flow of music. Nellie leaned against her. Katie had no idea when her guests came downstairs. She didn't notice them. She was only vaguely aware that many of her neighbors were standing outside the window.

Sunset came and the *Yarwoo*, as always, flew to Mr. Ovani, touching him lightly and then flew to Mrs. O'Leary. The touch of her wings was longer this time, like a lingering caress, thanking her for the sunlight.

Katie's skin tingled where the *Yarwoo* touched her. The neighbors slipped away, no one making any comments about what they might have seen in the parlor, including a cow, or about the beautiful creature who sang like one of God's angels. Katie didn't even cross herself at the fear of blaspheming. She couldn't imagine the angels sang any sweeter.

Mr. Szmch didn't complain that his supper was late.

Weeks slipped by. Katie thought it odd that her dresses had somehow gotten larger. She rarely got up before dawn to do any cleaning, except for the back parlor. That room was kept spotless. It was where the *Yarwoo* lived.

Sometimes Mr. Szmch got his supper; sometimes he didn't. He didn't complain, or maybe she just didn't hear him. It seemed she only had eyes and ears for the *Yarwoo*. Many times when it went to bed, so did she. There seemed little reason to stay up. Sometimes she ate; more often not.

Mr. Marlet fed himself, making trips to the barn after sunset.

Nellie took care of Mr. Longger, giving him oats and hay. She never said if the cow talked to her. Didn't matter.

So little seemed to matter except the *Yarwoo*. Katie could feel, in some way, its' growing joy as the pregnancy continued. The *Yarwoo* always stroked Katie's cheek before going to bed in the carved walnut box. It reinforced a bond between them.

September came. One morning Katie got up at dawn and knew, without being told, the *Yarwoo*, was no longer in the house. "Mr. Ovani!"

An image shimmered in front of her. Like Mr. Ovani had been before, all energy with little form. *Forgive this appearance, Mrs. O'Leary, but I am far away. I take the Yarwoo to a place where she can give birth and be safe.*

"I want to say good bye!"

The Yarwoo have no concept for good bye. She appreciates all you have done.

"Will I ever see her again?"

Perhaps. But not soon. She will give birth to three young very soon now. She will have to focus all her attention on them.

Mrs. O'Leary noticed for the first time, the weather had started to turn cool. Her neighbors stood outside the window. They did not know the *Yarwoo* was gone. Not one of them had spoken a single word to her about the singing, or the incredible colors that danced across the walls. Nor did it seem they ever told anyone else about what went on in her house. No one, other than neighbors, ever waited outside the window.

She walked over to the window and quietly closed it. The people gathered around understood and slowly drifted away.

Katie looked past the back parlor. Her house was truly filthy. She had not cleaned in weeks. She held up her hand and realized how very thin she had become. She could not remember when she had last been to the green grocer or the butcher. Nellie brought food sometimes. Mrs. O'Leary didn't always bother to eat that.

The *Yarwoo* was gone. Katie felt a fatigue that was nearly overwhelming, and she felt as though she was waking from a dream, a dream of beauty, and love. But dreams were, by definition, fleeting. A pause between the reality of daylight.

When had she last bathed? She actually couldn't remember.

She rarely bathed in the morning, but she picked up her robe, and a change of clothing and went up the backstairs to the bathroom. Her copper-colored hair was stringy and unkempt. So unlike her.

She took a long bath and dressed with care in one of her best dresses. It certainly was a bit large on her, but it would do. Putting her hair up, a single curl escaped. Katie let it be, resting on her shoulder. She settled a wide cream colored hat over her copper curls and picked up her silver handled walking stick. She had not left the house in weeks. She would walk to the bakery and buy some bread and several sticky buns. They might even have hot tea available. The bakery had a few tables there where an unescorted woman could sit and eat.

The dream was over. Time to return to the daylight of reality, to the life she had suspended. She would always, though, remember the beautiful colors and the soaring majesty of the music. They would live in her mind forever.

And in her dreams. She knew for the rest of her life her dreams would be threaded with colors beyond words and music beyond description.

Not in My House

"Will that be enough?" Mrs. O'Leary asked Merapet, the large grey Cat. She'd been pouring fresh skimmed cream into the loveliest container Katie has ever seen. It was brilliant red glass, or maybe it was a carved out jewel.

Merapet had brought it to carry the cream back to the heir of Hisrow Empire, the Gorset, who looked like a large calico kitten.

Hisrow wasn't the full name of the alien empire; something came after Hisrow, but it was a sound between a meow and a hiss, and the universal translator couldn't do anything with it. Katie just called it the Hisrow Empire. Actually she only called it that to herself and to Mr. Ovani.

Merapet had not been pleased the one time Katie had referred to the feline empire just as the Hisrow Empire. The hair on the back of large grey Cat's neck had risen alarmingly. After a moment, though, her fur settled back down. Katie had been glad of that. Merapet was part of a security team that protected the young heir to the throne. Merapet was trained in many ways of killing. Katie had no desire to be on the receiving end of any of them.

After her fur had settled down, Merapet had licked her paw a little, the gold tips of her claws showing, and had said in a soft, but friendly way. "I understand the full name of our empire is a little difficult for humanoids to pronounce."

Mr. Ovani later explained that using only part of the name was insulting. Since then, Katie had avoided using any form of the name.

Merapet was willing to overlook any minor misunderstanding between them as Katie had helped save the young heir to the throne, standing side-by-side with Merapet fending off what looked to be a large renegade Cat and two wolves who had been trying to recapture the bedraggled kitten.

Recovering in her kitchen, the kitten had tasted cream for the first time. Now By Royal Decree, Mrs. O'Leary was an official Provender to the Royal House of Hisrow. That basically meant Merapet came to Earth every couple of weeks to pick up a supply of fresh cream. The Gurset would have liked it more often, but his physician had decreed cream was a treat the kitten could have only when he earned it.

According to Merapet, the Royal Household was quite pleased with this as the Gurset's behavior had much improved after his time on Earth. Mrs. O'Leary thought the desperate days the kitten had spent on the streets of Chicago had helped him see how very lucky he was.

Very few in the Royal Household knew of the kidnapping of the heir by their ancient enemy. If it had become widely known, there would have been interstellar war. Best most everyone thought the heir had gone on a retreat to contemplate his August future. That also helped explain his subdued manner when he returned.

Merapet said the Gurset was returning more and more to his lively, outgoing self, but she doubted he would ever forget the dark days spent alone, hungry and threatened. The one good thing to come out of that desperate time, according to him, was cream.

"Just a bit more," Merapet said. "He has been very well behaved lately."

Mrs. O'Leary tipped the rest of the cream, from the neighbor's cow, into the beautiful jar. Merapet closed the jar with something that had to be a large jewel.

The back door slammed closed. Merapet immediately dropped down to four legs, her jeweled universal translator swinging around her neck like a necklace. Merapet had been standing on her back legs. Mrs. O'Leary had explained the house rules when Merapet had first come to Earth looking for the Gurset: Merapet had to act like a normal, if rather large, cat, in front of any other humans.

"Auntie!" Nellie called.

"In the kitchen." Katie draped a towel over

the jeweled container.

Tall, and with a teenage awkwardness, Nellie strode into the large kitchen, her long brown skirt swirling at her ankles. "Pa wants to know when you're gonna need me next week. He wants me to start helping out Mrs. Smith with her baking every morning. She's selling her pies over at the pub now."

"In the morning? You mean before you go to school?"

"Nah. Pa says schooling's not so important for me. Mrs. Smith gonna need me most of the morning."

Mrs. O'Leary's mouth set in a hard line. "You know your ma would have wanted you to finish high school. Your Pa knows that to."

"Ma's been dead since I was five."

"Doesn't matter. She set a profound importance on education. Even for girls. Your Pa knows that. Your two brothers are almost done with high school. They'll be going into trade soon."

Katie shifted uncomfortably. "Pa says we need the money."

Mrs. O'Leary had more than enough money, but knew better than to flash it around. Officially she ran a boarding house for some down-and-out types, which the aliens certainly were. Except for Mr. Ovani.

Not that the neighbors, or even Nellie, didn't realize something was very different at Mrs.

O'Leary's Boarding House. Especially since the *Yarwoo's* time some three months ago. Still no one spoke of that time. Not her neighbors, nor Nellie. It was as though that time, those months, were a contained secret that could never be spoken of for fear that the memories would vanish. No one wanted to lose the memories of the beautiful colors or the sweet singing.

"I'll talk to your pa," Mrs. O'Leary said firmly. "I've set aside a little money in case it was needed for your education. I know what your ma wanted."

Nellie stood still. "You sure? I would kinda like to finish high school."

"And maybe more," Mrs. O'Leary said quietly. She'd always made sure Nellie's helping her out didn't interfere with her school work and that it brought in enough money so Nellie's pa wouldn't have any reason to say no. He wasn't a hard, or unkind man, but he didn't see much use for education for girls beyond a simple point of reading and basic mathematics. Most men didn't. Well, even most women didn't, truth be told.

"I'll talk with your pa. Tell him I'll be by later today. We'll work something out."

"I'd be grateful, auntie."

Katie nodded. "You run along. I've got some chores to finish up."

Nellie looked down at Merapet. "That's one big cat you've got there." She gave her aunt a shy, grateful smile and went down the long corridor towards the front door.

Merapet stood up gracefully. "If there is financial difficulties...? We owe you a debt beyond merely words. You have but to tell me what you need. Ours is a wealthy empire."

Awkward sometimes, that universal translator. Katie wished Merapet hadn't heard that. "No. I'm fine. I just have to be careful people don't see me spending too much money. Could lead to difficult questions. Or even violence."

"Do you need security? I can have some of our trained guards..."

The thought of trained attack cats living in her house gave her a shiver. She'd seen Merapet in action. No neighbor's dog would survive. "No. I'm fine. I very much appreciate your offer, though. I just have to talk some sense into that girl's father."

Merapet smiled, showing gold tipped fangs. "You will please let us know if there is any way we can be of service. A one-sided debt is always awkward."

"Hardly one-sided, and hardly a debt. I just stood beside you and swung a bat. Mr. Ovani settled the matter."

Merapet took the jeweled vessel. "I must talk with him a bit before I leave."

"He's in his room. Or at least I think he is. I'm not always sure he is here when he seems to be here, if that makes sense."

"With an Ovani, yes, that makes complete sense. And thank you again for capturing the cream."

Mrs. O'Leary had tried to explain how cream came from a cow that was milked, but it came out through the universal translator as something quite different. Universal translators had little experience with a world as backward as Earth.

As far as money went, Katie had never melted down the gold coins Merapet had insisted on giving her after they had saved the Gurset. The coins were just too beautiful. Very few planets among the stars used any sort of hard currency. Mostly the interstellar economy ran on credits. Katie had no idea what that meant. She understood, though, that coins were rare and usually quite pretty. Those of the Hisrow Empire, so well-known for its elegance, were the most beautiful she had ever seen.

Katie stood for a bit longer in the kitchen. Soon she'd have to start working on fermenting more of the sauce Mr. Marlet had taken a liking to. Something he had learned about when he visited another six legged cat in Norway. Vile stuff in her opinion. Fermented fish. Still Mr. Marlet paid extra for her to make it, so she did. It needed several days of fermenting to get it right.

Today wasn't one of the days Mr. Ovani needed supper. Hard to call shimmering silver

metal marbles food, but that was what he ate.
Sort of. Actually Katie wasn't sure what he did
with them. She kinda doubted they were food in
any normal sense of the word.

She needed to get going; she'd been a bit lazy
this morning. Walking out to the side porch, she
gave a good kick to the wood storage box with
her thick leather high top boots. She waited a
bit, hearing skittering sounds, then lifted the lid.
Nothing moved on the top of the wood pile. The
kick always drove the various critters to the
bottom. She'd a cousin who had died after being
bit by a rat sitting on the top of the wood in the
wood box. Katie didn't take chances.

She chose two small logs, carrying them into
the kitchen. She didn't have a lot of cooking to do
today; they should do. She opened the door to the
firebox on her cast iron stove and tipped them in,
sending a shower of sparks flying upward. She
always kept a low fire going, even in summer, to
make it easier to get the logs going for cooking.
Too much work it was to start a fire from scratch
every day.

Still, it would be a few minutes until the heat
was appropriate for boiling Mr. Marlet's sauce.
She had time to sit a spell and sip some tea.

She poured a cup from the kettle simmering
on the stove. Plenty hot enough for the relatively
mild November weather. Walking into the front
parlor, she sat down with a sigh.

Almost immediately she heard Mirapet and

Mr. Ovani coming down the stairs. It was easy to tell it was them. Mirpet's steps were light and graceful; Mr. Ovani, in his human form, always used a cane.

Also none of her other current boarders walked down the steps. Mr. Szmsch very rarely left the redesigned room with its water environment. Mostly just on the Sundays when all her guests gathered in the front parlor. He clamored down the stairs with his tentacles, an oil skin held around him to keep the moisture in close. Mr. Marlet didn't seem to use the stairs; he just showed up in the parlor. Disconcerting that was, but however he travelled, he didn't seem to use the stairs. Her newest guest, Mr. Yetvi, was a snake-like creature. He slid down the handrail.

Katie had no idea why, when Mr. Ovani took human form, he chose to have a cane. It didn't matter really. It was a very nice cane. It just seemed a bit odd. He certainly didn't need it to walk.

Merapet and Mr. Ovani finished whatever silent conversation they were having. Merapet gave Mr. Ovani a slight formal bow, smiled at Katie, and left carrying the jeweled container as though it contained the finest nectar of the gods. It was just the Johnson's cow's cream. The back screen door closed quietly as Merapet left.

Mrs. O'Leary knew from past experience once Merapet was clear of the door, she would drop to all fours again, but the cream would go before her on a small anti-gravity sled, low to the ground where it would be difficult to see. Once in the old barn at the back of the property, she would load it onto her interstellar craft and leave as soon as it was dusk. The Hisrow Empire had developed some sort of invisibility cloak. Not complete invisibility, but in the fading light of the sun, the ship would never been seen. Mrs. O'Leary had even watched for it and hadn't seen it.

Always good to be sure. Earth wasn't ready to learn of who, and what, her boarders were. No one traveled back and forth to the stars during the day.

Mr. Ovani lingered in the front parlor. If he were human, Katie might have thought he was uneasy. *How could someone as powerful as he be uneasy over anything?*

"Mrs. O'Leary?" Mr. Ovani finally began. "I will be leaving for a time. Not long, I hope."

"Why is that, Mr. Ovani? No problem with my cooking, I hope?"

Mr. Ovani smiled. "No, of course not. Your cooking is excellent. The sauce is just as I like it." His cane shifted a little, making a small swirling sign. "It is...business. I must be somewhere else for a time. That is all."

"Some other world needs you?"

"It is more...well, it is a bit too difficult to describe. But I will be back. Mayhap seven of your sun's cycles?"

"You mean seven years?" Mrs. O'Leary was clearly upset.

Mr. Ovani thought about it. "No, no. Umm, seven days. Maybe ten. Not more than that. I'm sorry if I used the wrong words."

Mrs. O'Leary relaxed. She could manage seven days without Mr. Ovani. She was so used to him helping if anything went wrong, as it surely did sometimes, she did not want to try managing her boarding house without him. Although they had never directly discussed it, she was sure Mr. Ovani was here to protect Earth. It was very reassuring.

"Merapet will be coming by most days," Mr. Ovani added.

Katie smiled. "I think I can manage a few days without you."

"It is best." Mr. Ovani's tone was firm.

Katie shrugged. She didn't mind the grey cat's company. "If you believe it is necessary."

"It could be."

That was vague, even for Mr. Ovani. And why might it be necessary? Did he know something? Surely if there was any possibility of trouble, he wouldn't leave.

Would he?

Mr. Ovani turned to back upstairs.

"You know you can stay downstairs if you'd like. I prefer my...guests...to remain upstairs only because I worry about someone seeing them.

You look like...well, a handsome human."

Mr. Ovani turned and smiled slightly. "I am more comfortable in my room."

"Is it anything I've done?"

"No, definitely not, Mrs. O'Leary. It is just I am more comfortable in my natural state and I can communicate with others more easily."

Mrs. O'Leary had never thought of that: how did Mr. Ovani communicate with others of his kind? After a moment she decided she didn't want to think too much about it.

"As you wish, of course. I just wanted you to know that you are always welcome downstairs."

At least when he was looking like a human. She didn't feel she needed to add that. She left for the kitchen. Time to get some cooking done.

Tonight wasn't one of the nights Mr. Yetvi needed supper. He ate supper only on Monday, Wednesday, and Friday evenings. She wasn't sure what he ate. His meals came in containers that were sealed. All she had to do was put the sealed container in a low heat oven for fifteen minutes, moving it around occasionally so the heat spread through the whole container. His grocer, another snake, brought the food every Sunday night. The boxes were kept in the ice box in the barn.

Chapter 2

Three days it had been since Mr. Ovani left.
Mrs. O'Leary found herself wondering when he
would get back and what he was doing. She
knew whatever he was doing, it was likely
beyond any of her imagining, but she still
wondered. Was he helping some other world?
Was there some political crisis on his home
world? Was there a war somewhere he was
mediating? He could do that with all his power.

Merapet had stopped by yesterday to see if
everything was going well. She had arrived just
after the sun set and left an hour or so later. The
large grey Cat seemed to be listening for
something, or maybe watching for something
Katie couldn't see. It made a person uneasy, it
did. Katie had trouble getting to sleep. She
wondered if she was letting her imagination get
out of hand just because Mr. Ovani wasn't
around.

The day had gone by quietly. The sun had set
and Katie was washing out the thick glass
bottles to return to the Johnson's for more milk
when she heard slithering on the staircase
handrail. Mr. Yetvi.

Katie wiped her hands on her apron and went
into the hallway between the front parlor and
the kitchen. Mr. Yetvi was dressed for travel,

which meant he was wearing his hat, a short round brimmed top hat. It looked a bit odd, a snake wearing a hat, but that was what he was wearing when he had arrived.

"Are you leaving, Mr. Yetvi?"

"Hmm, yesss. Right now."

"This is very sudden. Is there a problem?" He had only been here three weeks.

"What mean you – what problem?"

"Is the room not acceptable? Have I done something wrong with your food?"

"Room most unusual, very quaint. I like it. Food burned sometimes, but I eat it. Unusual flavor. I think burned sometimes is good."

"Why are you leaving?" Mrs. O'Leary decided to be direct.

"A problem. A bad...you do not have the right words."

"I don't understand."

"You aren't supposed to," Mr. Yetvi stated firmly. "If all is good enough, I will send for my things."

"If what is good enough?" Mrs. O'Leary began to worry a bit more.

"If you survive. Or if the house is still standing."

"Why should my house not be standing? Why might I be killed?"

"You will see. Must go now. No idea when they arrive."

Mrs. O'Leary tried to step in front of him to get more answers but the snake was too quick. He slithered around her and zipped down the hall faster than she could run after him. Katie thought the door might stop him, but then remembered she had unlatched the small door earlier in case Merapet came back.

The snake was out of the house with only his hat knocked slightly askew, slithering through the grass in the back yard. She deliberately kept the grass a bit long to hide things like snakes, or the big cockroach she'd had for a time. She could see the very top of Mr. Yetvi's hat as he made for the barn. No point in chasing him further. If he had decided to leave, he would have transportation waiting. She hated being in the barn when the roof slipped sideways and a ship took off. Unnerving it was with all the weird lights.

Besides if he wasn't going to talk, there wasn't a lot she could do about it. She could threaten to step on him or stab him, or even use the baseball bat, but he was a paying guest. That seemed quite rude.

She was getting truly worried. What the hell was going on? Oh, bother, now she would have to say the rosary as penance for swearing. Hail Mary...no, she'd do penance later, she needed to figure out what was going on first.

She stood in the kitchen rerunning what the snake had said: a problem was coming and it

would be here soon. A problem that might kill
her and might also destroy her house.

That wasn't good.

But why would anyone come here – to her
house – and cause trouble? She took in all types
of aliens; she didn't discriminate against any
species. No one should be angry at her.

She wished Mr. Ovani were here. He'd be able
to sort it out; she was sure of that. But he wasn't.
She was on her own. All right. Use logic. What
could be the reason any one might have to
destroy her house or kill her?

She shifted from one foot to the other,
pondering.

Could someone be trying to escape to Earth
pursued by people who didn't want that person
to get to her house, which was known to be a safe
haven for all types of aliens? Was the snake
concerned about a fight ending up in her house?
That didn't make sense. Mr. Yetvi couldn't know
about a chase somewhere in space.

Well, maybe he could. Since she started
taking in alien boarders, she'd seen things more
wondrous than communication over great
distances. But still the most Mr. Yetvi could
know was that some person was trying to get to
Earth to claim sanctuary at her house. He
couldn't know whether or not that person would
actually make it and that the conflict would take
place in her house.

Unless Mr. Yetvi could see the future.

That didn't seem likely. Unless he was similar to Mr. Ovani, which he wasn't. He was a snake. Literally. And he had said "might", so he didn't know for sure. So, something might happen, maybe was even likely to happen, but not that it would absolutely happen.

Mrs. O'Leary began to pace, worried about how much time she had before this problem, whatever it was, destroyed her house and maybe killed her. She abruptly stopped; pacing was a useless drain of energy. She needed to focus on what she knew.

Which was precious little. Basically someone was coming here, to this house, and that person, or persons, could – would likely – create a substantial problem.

Why? Was it something in her house? What could there be in her house that was worth anything to someone from the stars?

Nothing really. It didn't make any sense. She played no part in any world's politics. Yes, she had helped save the heir to the Hisrow Empire, but it was more Merapet and Mr. Ovani who had saved the kitten. She had played a very small part. She couldn't imagine anyone looking for vengeance on that. And besides almost no one else knew about that.

Katie stared out the back window. Mr. Yetvi had made it to the barn; she heard Mr. Longger talking to him. They were far enough away that she couldn't hear what Mr. Yetvi was saying. Mr.

Longger's voice, sounding more than a little like the lowing sounds of the cow he looked like, was too indistinct for her translator to pick up.

Was this problem the reason Mr. Ovani had left? He wouldn't do that. Surely with all his power, he had nothing to fear.

Whatever this problem was, it must have developed after he left. Was someone waiting for him to go, before…well, before doing whatever it was they planned? If that was the case, it didn't matter. Mr. Ovani wasn't there.

She needed to focus on the problem at hand: what was in her house that was of any value to someone from the stars?

It took Mrs.O'Leary only a moment more to realize what was the likely source of the problem: Mr. Szmch. He had ruled an empire, been disposed, and now was living in her second bathroom.

It was like having the deposed Emperor Ferdinand of Austria living in her house. Only more so. From what she understood Mr. Szmch had ruled over several planets not just one country. People didn't always like deposed emperors. Actually frequently many people didn't like deposed emperors, that's how they came to be deposed.

Katie went up the back stairs and tapped on Mr. Szmch's door. "May I come in?"

Mr. Szmch had two rooms really; the outer room, which was rather small and rarely used for anything with a small table and one small chair, and a very large bathroom which took up most of the original room.

Mrs. O'Leary had a carpenter and a plumber construct the large second bathroom. They both thought it very odd that someone with only five bedrooms would need more than one bathroom, but they built the room and ran the plumbing. Mr. Szmch supplied the force field that kept all the hot water and moisture contained within the room.

"Is that you, Mrs. O'Leary?" the metallic sound of Mr. Szmch's translator replied.

"Yes, Mr. Szmch. I'd like to talk to you." Katie wanted to talk to him face-to-face.

Not that he had a face in any way a human would. Still she wanted to talk to him face to whatever. She didn't want to stand outside the door shouting. If nothing else it was an issue of etiquette.

"Is that really necessary, Mrs. O'Leary?"

"I believe it is."

There was a shifting sound, some squishing that she didn't want to think too much about, and the door opened. "Come in quickly, I don't want to lose too much humidity."

Thinking of the hallway carpet, neither did she.

Slipping into the room, she caught her breath. The humidity was very, very high. Created difficulty in breathing, it did.

Mr. Szmch flowed, squished, and wiggled around. There didn't seem to be a good word for how he moved. Part of it was the tentacles. Lots of them. Lots more than an octopus even.

"Mr. Szmch, it has come to my attention that my house might be in danger. Would you know anything about that?" Katie had always been a direct woman.

Mr. Szmch thrashed out several of his tentacles. Katie took a quick step back to the door which was way too close. "It is not your businesssss!" he shouted. Actually, he gurgled; the translator changed the gurgles to human shouting.

So he did know. Katie stood up straight and took a step forward. "It most certainly is my business. This house is my business."

Two more tentacles joined the first three. They were waving right in front of Mrs. O'Leary's face. She didn't back down. "I take it you know what I am talking about."

The tentacles retreated a bit and twisted together in slippery, unhappy, wet knots. "Assassins come to kill me. My people want me back, but others want me dead, so I can never return. Yehvey was one of my personal servants. He came to tell me my people want me back. The usurper's eggs are cold. No one is happy."

She really didn't want to think about Mr. Szmch having warm eggs. Who was Yehvey? Oh, Mr. Vetvi. The snake.

"Several members of my royal guard are coming to protect me, to take me home where I belong. The assassins are ahead of them. My guards won't be here soon enough. I soooo want to go home, return to the wide oceans where I was laid as a sweet, warm egg."

So there was a race up in space. If the assassins got here first, there was going to be a conflict in her house. Maybe even if the assassins got here too soon after the royal guard she'd have a fight in her house.

"You should have told me this! You should have warned me!" Mrs. O'Leary was rather angry. If she had more time she could have told Merapet to get Mr. Ovani back. Or even just having Merapet would be helpful.

"Why tell you? There is nothing you can do. We must hope my guards get here first."

"Maybe." Mrs. O'Leary paused for just a moment. It didn't have to come to a fight that might destroy her house. All they wanted was Mr. Szmch. Really. They just wanted this octopus person, who was far from a polite guest.

But he was her guest. Katie felt a little ashamed at the thought that had flitted through her mind briefly. It didn't matter that Mr. Szmch was an octopus sort of thing or not. He was her guest, her boarder.

She looked on all her boarders as guests. People, well, Americans at any rate, didn't let someone walk in and kill a guest. It just wasn't done. So a fight it would be.

How could she defend her house?

The answer depended on how the assassins planned on killing Mr. Szmch. From what Mr. Ovani said, no one can use advanced weapons on Earth. Was that just an agreement that a group of assassins might choose to ignore? Or was there some way to make sure no advanced weapons were used? Mrs. O'Leary had no idea. The bounty killer had certainly used an advanced weapon.

"You should have told me this!" Katie repeated crossly. "You are a guest in my house."

The tentacles, and it was now eight of them, waved about her in consternation. "I do not want to die! Not here, not so alone!"

"Well, we'll see what we can do about that," Mrs. O'Leary returned. "How will they try to kill you?" she asked.

"I do not know. So many ways to kill. So many ways to die."

"Not so much here on Earth," Mrs. O'Leary said firmly. "Can they use weapons they bring from home?"

"Home?"

"Your planet," she snapped. Mr. Szmsch might have warm eggs, but he was certainly not particularly bright.

"No, no. It is forbidden."

"Will these assassins use them anyway?"

The tentacles finally drew back as though he needed them to think. Maybe he did. "I am not sure, but very unlikely. No one wishes to make the Ovani angry."

So they might have a chance. A small chance, but still. What were the human ways to kill: guns, knives...fire – fire would be bad. Very bad. What else? Poison? Club him to death? Mrs. O'Leary thought about it. That pretty much summed it up.

Not necessarily. There was a nagging in her mind but she couldn't think clearly. It was all this steam, her blouse was stuck to her chemise, which was stuck to her corset. She was dripping sweat. No wonder she couldn't think straight.

"You cannot help me, Mrs. O'Leary. They are very deadly, these assassins. They will only send the best."

To kill an unarmed octopus in her second bathroom? It wouldn't need high level assassins. She could do it herself: just shut off the hot water.

Shut off the hot water.

That was it! Mr. Szmch had to have constant hot water to survive. The assassins would know that.

Even as she thought it, the hot water began to fizzle and very slowly the water stopped flowing.

"AAAGH!"

"It can't be that bad yet, Mr. Szmch!" Katie said firmly. "I have another bathroom." How had they shut off the water? Was there no water in the whole house? Or did the real bathroom still have water.

"Stay here." Katie slipped out, opening the door as little as possible. Her leather shoes were soaked and she slid slightly on the wood floor until she reached the carpet in the middle of the hallway. She scuffed her shoe soles dry, then crossed the hall to the other bathroom and turned on the hot tap. Water flowed. Thank Jesus! Then it slowed to a trickle and stopped.

Mrs. O'Leary could think of several very bad words to say but she didn't want to have to confess to saying those words to Father O'Malley.

Water. She needed water—hot water, steam really. What did she have? How could she create steam? If there was no water in the bathroom there wouldn't be any in the kitchen either.

She did have ice though. The ice man had just come by so she had a large block of ice in the ice box. She had a stove. Maybe she could keep Mr. Szmch alive for a while. At least until his guards came. She had to at least try.

She banged on the bathroom door. "How long until your guards get here?"

"AARGH, I will DIE!! DIE in this place of horrors!"

Her house wasn't that bad. "HOW LONG?"

"I will not survive once my *ogemt* is dry."

The universal translator couldn't tell her

what an *ogemt* was and Mrs. O'Leary wasn't sure
she wanted to know. Could have something to do
with his eggs. She didn't want to know about
that.

"They are here."

Mrs. O'Leary jumped sideways. Spinning she
looked for something to use as a weapon.

"Mrs. O'Leary!"

Katie looked down. It was Mirapet. Even
standing on her back legs, the grey cat was
barely taller than her waist. "How? Why are you
here?"

"I've been here since yesterday. Rumors fly
through the stars. Ovani heard them and told me
to watch out for you. He knows they will come to
kill the *ittilig*."

"*Ittilig*?"

"The deposed ruler of *Qzund*."

Katie still looked a bit blank.

"You call him Mr. Szmch."

"There is going to be an assassination
attempt? And Mr. Ovani left?"

"He had no choice."

Katie would have a few choice words to say to
Mr. Ovani when he came back. Now however,
they had to save Mr. Szmch. "I have some ice –
frozen water --"

"The cold will kill him."

"I can melt it on the stove. I can create
steam."

Mirapet nodded. "Start that. I will remain here for now and guard the *Ittilig*."

Katie ran as fast as she could in her slippery leather shoes down the front staircase. She had just turned into the hallway that connected the front of the house with the kitchen when the front door exploded in. Thick oak it was, too. The door remained in one piece but the frame shattered. The small stained glass insert was in shards.

Katie was glad it was full dark outside and the gas lights in the hallway were turned down. She wouldn't want her neighbors to see what just walked in her house. Two upright lizards. Near seven feet tall they were. They crowded through the broken door and stood in the entryway, lifting their thick snoots to sniff.

She couldn't let them get upstairs. She had no idea how to beat them; doubted if she could, but if she could manage to keep them away from Mr. Szmch until his guards arrived it would be good enough. Surely his guards would be able to protect them.

The lizards' long heads turned towards the stairs. Katie picked up a vase a guest had given her that she had never liked. Heavy metal. She flung it with all her strength at the lead lizard's head. Hit him hard.

The head barely tilted back, but the lizard turned and looked at her. They both did. That could be a problem, even if it was what she wanted. Thinking quickly, she flattened herself against the wall.

"Afraid of me, are you?" she sneered and threw a book. She hated to do that; she liked books, but it was the only other thing she could quickly reach.

The lead lizard easily dodged it. He took two steps closing the distance between them. Katie leaned in closer to the wall, just beyond the gas jet for the wall sconce. The lizard's head darted towards her. Before his sharp fangs could snap at her head, Katie turned the gas jet up full. The hot flame caught the lizard full in his face.

The guttural scream was nothing human. The lizard staggered backwards, his webbed paws clawing at his face. The second lizard pushed his injured partner aside and lumbered towards her.

Jesus Christ. Holy Mary, mother of God. Not blaspheming, praying for help.

The first lizard crashed to the floor, his claws ripping a long gouge in the plaster. The second lizard stepped over his thrashing companion. Katie backed up into the kitchen. At least she had some pans there. And a little more room to move.

The lizard gave a low, guttural snarl and a violent hiss. "I will kill you and eat your eggs."

Katie's universal translator, which she wore as a necklace, translated the guttural grunts and snorts. "Damned if you will!" She was sure the priest would understand using profanity in this case. She'd have to change the situation, of course, when she confessed.

Katie didn't take her eyes off the large lizard as she reached for the large cast iron frying pan she always kept on the stove.

The monster lizard kept walking forward.

Katie picked up the pan and with both hands swung it with all her strength, hitting the lizard on the side of his head. He stumbled sideways. Katie backed up a few more steps. The lizard jerked upright again.

Katie wondered where Merapet was. She could use her help here.

"I do not have to kill you," he hissed. "The *ittilig* is dying upstairs. That is all that matters."

Maybe to him, but her house would get a definite black mark if one of her guests died here. Katie stepped forward, holding the heavy skillet. "How did you shut off the water to the house?" She didn't even know how to do it.

"Yehvi has been very helpful."

So truly a snake in the grass. Mr. Szmch thought Mr. Yehvi was one of is servants. Obviously he was mistaken in that.

The lizard stepped forward again, his mouth opening wide, his thick yellow tongue flicking out between razor sharp teeth. He kept his head back as his long, heavily muscled arms reached towards her. She wasn't going to be able to hit him in the head again.

Well, if not high, then aim low. She dropped down and nailed both his feet, one after the other, in rapid succession, with the edge of the heavy skillet.

The lizard's scream was more of fury than pain.

That wasn't good. Katie leaped back and held the skillet out in front of her. The lizard hissed, his orange eyes narrowing to slits. He lumbered forward, his teeth dripping.

And was abruptly taken down by a black cat the size of a lion. The very large, well-muscled cat tore into the lizard with a ferocity that might have been unnerving except if the cat hadn't been there, she likely would have ended up as lizard chow.

Katie wondered if this panther cat liked cream?

No time for that just now. She presumed the cat was either one of Mr. Smzch's guards or related to Merapet. She ignored the bloody, one-sided battle, and put the skillet back on the stove. Running to her ice box, she found the new block of ice; it was too big for her to pick up. She took one of the fire irons she used in the stove and beat the block of ice several times shattering it.

Taking the biggest chunks of ice, she got out her roasting pan and put it on the stove, dropping the chunks of ice in. She barely gave the wood box a decent kick before opening it.

Several things were still scurrying to the bottom as she pulled out a couple of large pieces of wood.

The large black cat dragged the now dead lizard to the far side of the kitchen. He padded down the hallway to finish off the first lizard.

Good riddance, Mrs. O'Leary thought. She never did cotton much to lizards. Wouldn't have thought she'd risk her life for an octopus type thing either. But that was different. He was a paying guest.

Mrs. O'Leary got a good fire going under the roasting pan. The black cat padded back into the kitchen.

"Need more help?" he asked. Obviously his universal translator had been preset for Earth. Merapet thought of everything.

"Not here. Please tell Merapet Mr. Szmch can come down now." She had a good head of steam on the pan. In the basement was some oil cloth. They could put the steaming pan of water on the floor and make a tent with the oil cloth right over it. That should keep Mr. Szmch damp enough until his guards arrived. She'd start a second pot of ice going just to be sure.

Chapter 3

"Are all humans like you?" Merapet asked, as several more lizards, Mr. Szmch's guard, wrapped him in a hot moisture cloth. A force field shimmered up around him. The octopus was positively purring. Who knew an octopus could purr?

"What do you mean?" Mrs. O'Leary asked as she went to get a mop and bucket. Keeping Mr. Szmch hot and damp had left rather a mess on her kitchen floor.

"Many beings in the galaxy would not risk their lives for another who is so different from them. You risked your life for the heir to our throne and now for the *ittilig*."

Mrs. O'Leary began to mop.

"No, no. You do not do such menial labor." Merapet meowed. She turned to the black lion and said something the translator did not recognize. The black cat scurried over and took over mopping the floor.

Truthfully, Katie was a bit tired. She gave up the mop without any protest.

"Come let us sit down in your parlor. You are obviously tired."

The largest lizard said something to Merapet, who replied in the same language. Translator simply hummed. Another language the translator did not recognize.

The large lizard turned towards Katie and spoke in a language the translator understood. "The Cat says that you saved our *Ittilig*?" The questioning aspect was clear in the translator.

"I didn't do much. Merapet's people killed the

assassins."

"She says you stopped the first assassin and slowed down the second enough to allow the *carzom* to kill it."

The *carzom* was obviously the large black lion. So Merapet had been aware of what was going on even while upstairs. That was reassuring.

"I didn't do much. Just slowed them down a bit."

The tallest lizard raised its head. "You are saying the Cat lies?" There was a definite undercurrent of threat in his tone, even through the translator.

"No," Merapet said firmly. "She is a modest being; that is all."

The lizard tilted his head as though that was an odd concept.

"I want to go HOME!" Mr. Szmch said. "NOW."

"Yes, your *ittilig* Majesty."

Mr. Szmch was picked up and placed on an anti-gravity sled. He, with his escort, left without a backward glance, or even a single good-bye.

Katie couldn't help but feel a little let down. She had risked her life for Mr. Szmch after all.

Merapet sighed a little. "They are not a species that understands gratitude or debt well. I will speak with the *Ittilig*, you will be compensated for your trouble.

Katie sighed as well. "That's not necessary. He paid well enough."

"It is most certainly necessary. If for no other reason than he put me and my household to some effort. We do not do that for just anyone."

"You were here to save Mr. Szmch?"

"Of course not. He could have been killed several times over and I would not have lifted one claw. The species is self-centered and arrogant. Szmch most of all."

"He was kind while here."

"He had nowhere else to go. He is arrogant, but not a fool. I have spent much of the last few days here keeping watch because of you, Mrs. O'Leary. We owe you too great a debt and our species acknowledges what is owed."

"My name is Katie," Mrs. O'Leary reminded her.

"What is Katie? I do not understand. You said before your name was Katie, but everyone addresses you as Mrs. O'Leary."

"Katie is a personal name. Only close friends and family use a personal name."

"Permow wanted you to know his name as well.

"Who is Permow?"

"The heir to the Hisrow Empire. He truly appreciates your hunting the cream for him." There was a sound after Hisrow and before

Empire but the translator didn't try to turn it into human words.

Katie smiled. "It is nothing," she said honestly.

Chapter 4

Mrs. O'Leary sat on the swing on the front porch. Mr. Ovani sat beside her, holding his silver and ebony cane. The swing swayed gently. It was a lovely night, a cool breeze had come up, but it was still tolerable. The widow, Mrs. Smith, paused on her walk to wave, but did not come up the steps. Mrs. O'Leary was grateful that her neighbor had finally understood that Mr. Ovani had no interest in her.

She smiled slightly thinking of the hysterics the poor woman would have if she saw some of the forms Mr. Ovani took. He was being kind to her, sitting there as though he were human. Made it easier to talk to him, it did.

And she wanted to talk to him. Had a bit of a bone to pick with him.

"You knew what was going to happen, didn't you?"

Mr. Ovani gently pushed the swing back and forth with his ebony cane. "You think I can see the future?"

"If you want to, yes."

The swing moved gently back and forth before he answered. "There is no such thing as a set future. Even five minutes from now, many things could happen. Many different things. Two carriages could crash right in front of this house. A bird could die. Or maybe not."

"There are many possible futures. That's what you're saying?"

"Yes."

"But you know what is most likely." Mrs. O'Leary didn't phrase it as a question.

"Sometimes," Mr. Ovani answered slowly. "Sometimes so many things are possible it is hard to know what will happen."

"You knew it was likely assassins would come here to kill Mr. Szmch."

"Yes."

"And you left because you of that. You chose not to be here." Again it was a statement.

The swing continued its gentle swaying. "It was not a matter of choice."

Mrs. O'Leary gave a very unladylike snort. "You left me to face them alone."

"No. I made sure Merapet would be close by."

"I thought you protected Earth."

"I do. These assassins would not have harmed Earth. They just came to kill the one you call Mr. Szmch."

"You knew I would not let them; you knew I would try to stop them."

Mr. Ovani smiled, his teeth even and white. "Yes, I did. I have a great deal of...respect...for your courage."

"Why couldn't you stay?" She needed to understand that. "If you had been here…"

Mr. Ovani shook his head. "I can protect Earth; I can stop those who would harm Earth, but a palace coup is not the same."

"Stop anyone who would harm Earth, or can you stop anyone who would harm humans?" Mrs. O'Leary settled her hands in her lap, the picture of a proper lady.

"I protect Earth," Mr. Ovani answered. "However, if many humans might be harmed, I can intervene."

"You helped when the Gurset was kidnapped."

Mr. Ovani sighed, a very human sound. "Once the heir had been found by his own people, and you were under attack, with the possibility of the harm to other humans, I intervened."

"But I could have been harmed when the assassins came to kill Mr. Szmch."

The swing moved gently back and forth as Mr. Ovani made no reply. "A single human," he spoke gently. "And truly I should not have intervened before. Merapet may have been able to save the Gurset on her own, particularly with you distracting some of the attackers. I went against…the rules."

"Who says? Who made up these rules?"

"I did; my people did."

"I don't understand." Mrs. O'Leary stared at her guest. Why would anyone make up rules to tie up their hands like that? Not that the Ovani had hands, but still...

"Long ago, my people had this very discussion," Mr. Ovani spoke softly. "We have power, power unmatched by any other species. Some of my people felt such power should be used to help those in need in the universe, some believed we should stop all wars and control violent behavior."

Mrs. O'Leary said nothing, but she began to understand the problem. She was wrong.

"Some of my people wanted this, but others felt very strongly we should limit ourselves to our home place. We have never been a species that liked to travel much into space. Our home...place...suits us."

Mrs. O'Leary wondered a little about this 'home place', but didn't want to interrupt him.

"It seems almost odd thinking back to that time. It was so long ago."

"What happened?"

"Some of my people felt very strongly about wanting to help the galaxy while others felt just as strongly that we should not meddle with others. Eventually, a war began."

"Jesus save us." Mrs. O'Leary had seen some examples of Mr. Ovani's power.

Mr. Ovani's lips tilted a little in what could be a mocking smile. "We have no deities. It might have been better if we did."

"What happened?"

"One of the problems with war, whether here on your planet or with our species: you cannot always see the consequences. War is so very...different from most other activities, even those of us who can most accurately gauge the future never saw...we never knew, or even guessed."

Mr. Ovani said nothing more for several moments as the swing moved back and forth, perhaps a little more quickly. "We are very different from most species. We do not die; we are not corporal beings. This war was really a flexing of...there is not good word in your language; it is too limited. Mayhap it is best described as a flexing of will. Our will displays as power. Sometimes very massive power."

"Something happened." Mrs. O'Leary laid a gentle hand on Mr. Ovani's for a brief moment, then the memory of the many things he could be made her draw her hand back.

"Yes, something happened. In a very large...flexing of will, a solar system was caught in the power surge. We found out later that one of the planets had been inhabited. A young culture, on the brink of space travel. We eliminated them entirely."

Mrs. O'Leary started to speak again, but stopped. There really weren't any words. Mr. Ovani was right. English could be very limited sometimes. The silence drew out. Such power. Such guilt.

"So...now we protect all young cultures. It is the only thing we thought we could do. We cannot go back and save that world, but we can protect others. However, we will not meddle in the politics of other cultures. We all agree on that now."

Mrs. O'Leary found tears welling up in her eyes, tears for a species she had never seen, would never see. It didn't matter; she could imagine all of Earth gone in an instant, nothing remaining. A tear slid down her cheek.

Mr. Ovani looked at her. "I'm sorry. I should not have told you."

Mrs. O'Leary shook her head. "No. It is best that I know. Now I understand you better." She touched the tear away with the back of her hand.

Mr. Ovani smiled slightly. "I do not believe any being has said that to me in all of my years."

Katie again lightly touched his hand. "It's getting cold; I think I'll turn in."

Mr. Ovani stopped the swing. He turned the hand that she lightly touched over and helped her to her feet. "Good night, Mrs. O'Leary. I will always protect you in what ways I can."

Katie understood. He would protect her, but he would never do so at the cost of interfering in other planets politics. Still, how often would a palace coup take place in her house?

She worried it might happen more often than

she wished. Earth did seem to attract the wrong type of people that was a fact.

A Request

All independent authors depend on reviews to help increase sales.

If you would take the time to write a review of this book, it would be greatly appreciated.

Please visit me on Facebook, www.facebook.com/wfhalsey, or check out my website: www.winifredhalsey.com where I have short stories available to read for free.